Tales of Tessagonia
Books 1-6

The Blazing Princess
Mirror
The Princess Test
Venom and Shadow
The Gloaming Realm
The Moon Prince

Mary W. Jensen

Contents

Introduction

I have my family to thank for these tales, particularly Elizabeth. I have eight siblings. Amazingly, seven of us had some level of interest in writing. My older sister Beki was always telling stories, and was a huge inspiration in my early desires to write. I don't have her talent for verbal storytelling, instead being drawn entirely to the written word. I wanted some encouragement and accountability and wanted to inspire that in my siblings as well. The other sibling most serious about writing was my sister Elizabeth. Together, in October 2006, we decided to start The Wilcox Writers. We had regular meetings, wrote newsletters, and shared our work. We had an online forum for those out of state to join in. In our very first meeting, we decided to do a fairy tale project. I wanted to do a Sleeping Beauty story. In March 2007, I finished that story, *The Blazing Princess*. I wrote the follow up, *Mirror*, in May that same year. I had notes for a third story, *Zuleika* (later to become *The Princess Test*).

I tried submitting my stories to a few places, but they were too long for short stories and too short to be novels. I didn't know what to do with them, so rather than continue with the series, they got pushed aside while I worked on my novels.

Fast forward to 2020. The Wilcox Writers had long fallen dormant, revived temporarily, then fallen to the wayside again. I had finished a novel, which went through many many revisions. I tried to get an agent or publisher, but the fantasy market is hard to get into it. So that got benched as well, and my other novels in progress suffered from my lack of self esteem. But a few things remained the same. My love for fairy tales and that sister/writer bond I had with Elizabeth. We wanted to collaborate again, so ended up starting Briarbook Lane—website, blog, and fairytale book club. Having our eye on all things fairytale, I suggested getting a workbook [1] Spellcraft: Write Like a Witch, which is all about writing fairytales. Approaching one assignment, I remembered I already had the framework for an original fairytale in my Zuleika story, so I used the opportunity to finally plot out and write the tale. Elizabeth was very encouraging in my return to this world, and has been a wonderful supporter of it ever since.

Publishing had changed, self-publishing was no longer looked down upon and was easier than ever. So I decided to revisit and revise my tales and publish them as novellas myself. Thus Briarbook Lane Press was born, and The Tales of Tessagonia began.

---

1. Book by The Carterhaugh School of Folkore and the Fantastic. https://carterhaughschool.com/

Timeline

RM (Rule of Man) marked the beginning of Man's rule in Tessagonia. This was followed by EU (Era of Unification). Here are the titles in chronological order.

The Gloaming Realm (0 RM)

The Moon Prince (1 - 21 RM)

Venom and Shadow (70 EU)

The Blazing Princess (70 - 88 EU)

The Princess Test (82 EU)

Mirror (72 - 92 EU)

Days of the Week

The seven days of the week are named for the seven muses.

Tinsday (Tesni)

Awnday (Anwen)

Kaladay (Kala)

Menerday (Meinir)

Gwynsday (Gwynaeth)

Enisday (Enid)

Crysday (Carys)

The Blazing Princess

Mary W. Jensen

Contents

The first rays of dawn burst through the window to shine directly upon her birth, illuminating hair the same red–gold as the rising sun. And so it was only natural that she was named after that which had blessed her: Aurelia.

Augustus and Lorelei, King and Queen of Vernissia, planned the unveiling of their heiress to be held in one month's time. Invitations went out to the neighboring kingdoms, including the mystical realm of Lesenti, home of the seven muses. Custom decreed that all royal born receive blessings from the muses.

The day before the grand event, the seven muses glided into the courtyard on their rainbow-hued pegasi. They were given a special wing of the guest manor.

The next morning, servants overheard bickering from the muses' quarters. Anwen, Kala, and Enid debated over whose sphere of influence was most important. Gwynaeth distracted the sisters with her playfulness, but the question remained in their minds.

At precisely the eighteenth hour, guests filed into the banquet hall. Tables lined the walls, filled with exotic fruits, succulent meats, shaped breads, and decadent desserts.

A long table sat above the rest, with the king and queen seated at its center. Two round tables graced the floor directly below it.

These three tables were covered in fine cloths and fresh flower centerpieces. Smaller tables were scattered throughout the hall.

The hosting couple stood, and King Augustus raised his hands in greeting. Visiting royalty took their seats at the long table as they were introduced. The children of these visiting monarchs circled one of the round tables.

King Augustus gestured toward the two empty thrones on his right. "These seats are reserved for the Sun God Bentos and the Moon Goddess Delwyn. May they continue to bless these allied lands of Tessagonia. Though they do not grace us with their presence today, I extend my appreciation to the attendance of their daughters, the Muses of Lesenti."

The muses nodded and took their places at the remaining round table. The king clapped his hands and ordered the festivities to begin. Gwynaeth, Tesni, and Carys went to the buffet. The other four sisters remained at their table, preferring servers to bring their food.

Meinir tipped her glass to her lips, wetting her mouth before addressing Anwen. "I overheard your argument this morning. Do you truly believe that beauty is greater than art?"

Anwen plucked a pink dahlia the same shade as her dress from the centerpiece. "Beauty is a driving force in any world. One bases the first opinion on looks. The ugly, undeserving of life, cannot survive the ridicule of their peers. Beauty is most important for those royal-born," she said, gesturing with the flower toward the royal table, "as beauty breeds trust and worship. The common man cannot look up to those who rule if he cannot stand to look at them at all."

Kala laughed. "You are besotted with yourself. Art is much greater than beauty, for art can create beauty where there is none, and reveal the flaws in that which is perceived to be perfect. Beauty eventually fades away, but art endures time. The only point I'll concede to Anwen is that both our spheres are better than Enid's. We make life worth living."

Enid listened thoughtfully, running her fingers along the hem of her silver sleeve. Their food arrived and she nodded her thanks to the servers. "What of you, Meinir? Surely you can't agree that one of their influences is better than the rest of ours."

The muse of elegance flipped back her long auburn curls. "They are right in that beauty and art enhance life, but those are not necessary for survival. The world is much safer for a person if she is not tripping over herself and klutzing into every object in sight." She arched an eyebrow at Anwen. "One cannot appreciate beauty if they are falling flat on their face." She looked up as a hand touched her shoulder.

"One must have compassion for those with less elegance than thyself," Tesni admonished as she lowered herself into her chair with her own plate. "I cannot see how you argue thus. All of our spheres are equal." She nodded to Carys and Gwynaeth as they returned to the table. "What is a life devoid of happiness or love?" She looked pointedly at each of her sisters. "We are all equal in the eyes of Bentos and Delwyn. We were not asked to come here to bless a child as competing sisters, but as complementing muses. Now let us stop the arguing and enjoy this pleasant feast."

Her sisters conceded and resumed their meal. Enid sawed a piece of venison. How can the spheres be equal, if without life then none else exists? I'll prove to them who has the greater influence, she thought.

After the meal, everyone moved to the ballroom. King and queen stood in front of their thrones. An elaborate bassinet lined with silk rested on the dais before them. Lorelei received her daughter and presented her to the crowd. "A single year ago, I believed I could not bear a child. Thanks to the blessing of the Sun God himself, I introduce to you Princess Aurelia, my daughter, heiress to the throne of Vernissia."

Applause filled the room. The queen kissed her daughter and laid her in the bassinet.

The priest took her place. The holy man dipped his fingers in rose oil and pressed them to the babe's forehead, lips, and heart as he prayed to their gods. "We give thanks to Bentos for the gift of this child. He has marked her with his light. May Bentos watch over her during the day, and Delwyn keep her throughout the night." He rose, bowed to the royal couple, and departed.

The king took his wife's hand, and they sat as one. A herald announced the proceedings of the evening. A harp ensemble would play, and between each dance a muse would come forth to bless the child. After the final muse gave her blessing, a song of farewell would play before the celebration came to an end.

Tesni was the first to ascend the dais steps. She took a green ribbon and tied one end to the hood of the bassinet, the other end left dangling above the child. The baby swatted at the ribbon just out of reach. The muse smiled. "I, Tesni, daughter of Bentos and Delwyn, gift Aurelia of Vernissia with compassion. She shall lend understanding to those who come to her." With these words, she waved her hands above the princess, for a moment encompassing the cradle in a green light. After curtsying to the royal couple, Tesni returned to the dance floor and the music resumed.

After Anwen gifted Aurelia with rosy beauty, Kala countered by blessing her with a passion for oil painting, to preserve that beauty around her. The night went on as Meinir and Gwynaeth gave their blessings of grace and optimism respectively.

When Enid's turn came, she strode to the dais. Her own silver ribbon joined the other five, and she smirked at the baby's excitement. She wove her spell above the child, her voice carrying throughout the room.

"I, Enid, daughter of Bentos and Delwyn, gift Aurelia of Vernissia with eighteen years of life. In her nineteenth year she shall die, poisoned by those very oil paints for which she has been gifted a passion."

By the time King Augustus lurched forward in protest, the spell had been sealed with silver light. Queen Lorelei held back sobs with a trembling hand.

Enid curtsied to the couple, a smug smile on her lips. As she turned to descend the steps, guards moved forward to stop her.

The King signaled them to stop and addressed the muse. "I don't understand why you've cursed our only child. I dare not cause you harm, but this cannot go without consequence. You are never to enter the kingdom of Vernissia again. We would rather risk an early death than be cursed with the certainty of one. Be gone."

Enid stopped once, in front of her shocked sisters. "I believe my point is proven. Life is the greatest sphere. If any of you had reversed your influence, the reaction would not be so severe. Good day, sisters." With those final words, she made her departure.

No one moved. The musty smell of despair filled the room, and the only sound was the queen's muffled sobs. A happy giggle and wave came from the bassinet, the princess unaware of her fate. The room watched as Carys stepped forward and knelt before the royal parents.

"I have not yet blessed the child. I have no way to reverse my sister's curse. However, I do believe I can modify it to be less tragic."

Tenderly, she tied her ruby red ribbon next to the silver one. "I, Carys, daughter of Bentos and Delwyn, gift Aurelia of Vernissia with the enduring power of love. Yes, she will be poisoned and enter the realm of the dead, but her body shall merely sleep. The gate will remain open for one to follow her into the spirit realm. True love can bring her back. But the way will remain open for only a short time. If she is not found, she shall die. Let love overcome death."

Shoulders still drooped, so Gwynaeth came to join her sister on the dais. "All is not lost. The muse of love has given you hope this night. Do not let despair darken these eighteen years. Let them be filled with joy. Continue your celebration, for this beautiful princess before us deserves no less."

The King nodded in agreement. "The muse of joy speaks wisdom. Let no one speak of the curse. Aurelia deserves a normal life, without undue burden or pity."

Kala danced her fingers across her harp strings, and soon the rest of the ensemble picked up the tune. Smiles returned and steps grew lighter, and the curse slipped to the back of their minds.

2

During the summer after Aurelia's seventh birthday, Vernissia hosted the ten-year-old twin princes of Arania. The rulers of both kingdoms observed how well Aiden and Shane took to the little princess. The King of Arania proposed a betrothal between their children. King Augustus agreed, in the hopes that it would facilitate a future romance and secure a future for their daughter. Aurelia would marry Aiden, the younger prince by one hour. Shane, heir to the throne, was already betrothed to Hannah of Kether.

Aurelia gave the princes a tour of the royal gardens. Two heads of ash brown followed the bouncy red-gold curls as they hopped across the stones in the creek, climbed a ginkgo tree, and played hide and seek in the rose maze. Repetitive squawking interrupted their play and drew them to the pond at the center of the maze. Shane arrived first to find a ruby-crested crane tangled in a net. Aurelia followed, tugging Aiden along behind her.

"Oh! Poor thing. We have to help." With complete disregard for her shoes, she splashed into the water.

Shane put his hand on her shoulder, holding her from going further. "Careful, Aurelia, that bird is as big as you are."

Aiden plopped down on the green-veined marble bench a few feet away and flicked a pebble into the water, startling the crane to flutter its wings. One wing flapped free while the other entangled further in the rope weavings. "How'd it get caught up in a net? The royal pond should be protected from poachers."

Shane slipped off his shoes and stockings and rolled up his silk pantaloons. "I don't think the net was meant for the bird. The tiles around that bench are wet and flaked with fish scale. Someone fishing left the net behind." He slowly waded toward the crane.

Aurelia took Shane's movement as permission. She splashed past him to stop a foot away from the bird. She looked it in the eye as she reached a hand up to caress the bright red feathers along the top of its head. The crane shuddered but remained still.

Shane released the breath he was holding and gently began untangling the net as the princess crooned soft melodies. As the last of the rope fell away, the young girl smoothed down way-ward feathers and stood on her toes to kiss the bird on its crest. The ruby-crested crane rubbed its beak on Aurelia's cheek, then Shane's, before flying off.

Aiden stood and stretched. "Another successful rescue, Auri. Add that to the rabbit caught in the hedge, the frog in the well, and the puppy with the injured foot. How many creatures will you have cared for by our next visit?"

She giggled and sloshed over to climb on the bench, where she leaned over to give Aiden a wet kiss on his cheek. "Maybe next time I'll be rescuing you." Violet eyes sparkling, she leaped down to run off into the maze. The twins dutifully followed.

In Aurelia's twelfth year, all the royal families of Tessagonia were invited to a grand ball in Senatin. Aurelia met with Hannah to rehearse for the ball that night. Hannah hustled her into the small dance hall, giggling as she updated her on the latest gossip. Shane and Aiden entered from the opposite side, the dance instructors behind them.

Hannah twisted a lock of hair around her finger as she watched the brothers being ushered to their starting positions. "I still don't see the point in a rehearsal dance. All of us have been gifted with elegance. Why practice?"

Aurelia grinned. "You're a year my senior and still don't understand? You can naturally dance with grace, but you must learn the steps. Now, don't keep Shane waiting." Her voice softened as she looked over at him. "He's danced this before. You'll get so caught up in his arms you'll forget all about the rehearsal and simply float across the floor."

Hannah's eyes shone, and her skin flushed as she looked to him. "He is wonderful, isn't he? You're right; I shan't keep him waiting."

Aurelia's smile faltered as she watched Hannah rush to Shane.

Aiden gave a quick squeeze to Aurelia's hand as they took position. He whispered a joke in her ear and she laughed, letting him distract her.

Fifteen-year-old Aurelia slipped her arms into the large smock as her oils were prepared and placed at a hand table beside her.

The attendants left the room, knowing she preferred to be alone as she worked. Aurelia began to add patches of color to the canvas.

A knock interrupted her before she could make much progress. Sighing, she set the brush aside and called out for whomever it was to enter.

Hannah rushed in and perched herself on a settee, glowing with excitement.

Aurelia quickly closed her mouth. A princess should not be gaping and staring. "What brings you here?"

"The date has been officially announced. The first day of spring, two years from now."

Aurelia waited a moment before prodding further. "The date for what?"

Hannah giggled. "My wedding, of course. It will take place in Arania, as that is where Shane will be crowned. Shane and I are visiting each kingdom to make the official announcement as a couple. I wanted to let you know first, before the banquet tonight."

Aurelia turned away with the excuse of covering her paints, while she bit her lip and took a trembling breath through the tightness of her chest. She knew this day would come, but wondered why it had to hurt so awfully. Once composed, she moved to sit beside Hannah. They talked about the duties that would come with being named queen, and how it would be to live in Arania. The older girl continually brought the conversation back to her betrothed - how regal and handsome he was, and how she looked forward to being his wife. Hannah's sister had married the year before and told her all the secrets of marriage. Aurelia blushed at the forbidden images of Shane that filled her thoughts. Hannah's excitement blinded her to Aurelia's discomfort.

Aurelia held back a sigh of relief as another knock came. Her breath caught when she saw her new visitor come through the door. Shane. His broad figure filled the doorway, but the light in his blue eyes filled her heart. He had grown in the seven months since she had last seen him.

He came over to the girls and put a hand on Hannah's shoulder. "Your presence is required in your room. An issue has arisen with one of your maids."

She nodded and hugged Aurelia, promising to speak more with her later, then left the room. Shane took her place on the settee.

Aurelia squirmed and looked down at her clenched hands. "I hear the date is set."

"Yes." His voice had deepened. "You know it's not my choice. This has been planned since we were children." He lightly pushed a lock of red–gold hair behind her ear. His fingers lingered to caress her cheek.

Aurelia turned her face into his hand, but kept her eyes averted. "Do you love her?"

"She is kind, sweet, and full of life. She brings joy to me."

"But do you love her?"

His hand withdrew. "I must take my leave, princess. There are matters to attend before dinner."

She squeezed her eyes shut until she heard the door close again. Aurelia stripped her smock and called for a servant to put away her paints. She dashed to her room, throwing herself on the large soft bed. "He's really going to marry her. I had hoped..." She shook her head. "Silly me. I'm a princess, with many blessings, but cannot neglect my given duties." Aiden came to her thoughts, so like Shane in looks, but so different in personality. She took a deep breath to compose herself. "I must be strong, like Shane, and accept my betrothal."

3

Hannah and her younger sister Natalia came to help Aurelia plan her big eighteenth birthday party. They had only six months to plan meals, choreograph her formal presentation, hire entertainment, and send out invitations. The girls sat on her bed, Natalia with a journal and charcoal to take notes as they talked, her chocolate brown hair already in twin braids, while Hannah worked on braiding Aurelia's hair for the night.

"Hannah, thank you so much for leaving Shane for a few weeks. You and Natalia have been a great help."

"I don't mind at all. A year from now we'll be sisters-in-law. I consider you a sister already, so I'm excited to be involved in your birthday plans."

Natalia set down the book and turned toward them. "Aurelia. Why are you waiting six months after your birthday to wed Aiden? Hannah married Shane the week after she turned eighteen."

"I don't mind waiting. It wasn't my plan, though; it was detailed in our betrothal agreement." She thought for a moment. "I've never thought about the reasoning behind it."

They heard a knock on the door. Aurelia's mother poked her head in before the girls could respond.

Natalia quickly stood and curtsied. "Greetings, Queen Lorelei."

The queen smiled and nodded to the visiting princesses. "Greetings, Natalia, Hannah. There are tarts and tea in the library if you'd like to go down."

The sisters acknowledged the dismissal and scampered out. Lorelei shut the door and sat next to her daughter on the bed. "I have something to ask of you. No, it's not a request; it's a command. You are to stop painting with oils."

Aurelia frowned. "You want me to stop painting? But it's my favorite pastime, and I'm in the middle of a new piece."

"Have you heard any talk from the townspeople or the servants?"

"No. What are they saying? Someone doesn't like my work?"

"It's not that. Everyone thinks your paintings are beautiful masterpieces. And I'm not saying that because I'm your mother. However, they are questioning why I ever let you learn to paint. They are worried about you."

"Worried about me? Why? Painting isn't dangerous at all. I love painting. How could anyone expect me to give it up?"

"I've wanted you to have a normal, happy life. I didn't want to shadow you with things out of your control. But it's time you know." Her mother took a deep breath and placed her hand on top of her daughter's. "At your unveiling, not all of your gifts from the muses were blessings. One was a curse. Enid only gifted you with eighteen years of life, prophesying that you would be poisoned by your own oil paints."

The princess paled and clenched her mother's hand. "Are you saying I only have six more months to live? But why the betrothal then?"

"Carys, muse of love, countered the curse. She said your body will not die, only sleep. Love would follow your spirit into the realm of death and bring you back. The betrothal to Aiden will ensure that. I don't know that we can prevent it, but we have to try. Which is why I need you to stop painting." Tears slipped unheeded as she cupped her daughter's cheek. "I don't want to risk losing you."

Aurelia threw herself into her mother's arms and they held each other tight. The daughter took a shaky breath and whispered her consent. "I'll stay away from the oil paints." She pulled back and blinked past a film of tears. "May I still paint using other mediums?"

"Of course, if that would make it easier for you."

Aurelia said goodbye to her mother, then reflected by herself for a few minutes. She had heard tales of how beautiful and wondrous the muses were. She found it hard to believe one would do something so malicious. Why her, when all the other children had received only gifts?

When she finally joined the others in the library, Hannah and Natalia greeted her as joyfully as always. Aurelia considered talking to them about the curse, unsure if they knew of it, but decided not to. If this birthday did end up being her last, it should be a momentous and joyous one. Resolved to make this her best birthday ever, she cheerfully threw herself into the party planning.

Pleased with the plans made that week, Aurelia embraced the sisters before they went their separate ways. Natalia left for Kether, and Hannah prepared her carriage to return to her husband in Arania. Aurelia stopped Hannah before she climbed in, handing her a note to deliver once she arrived home.

Dearest Aiden,

We are to be married in one year's time, yet have not spent more than a week together since childhood. I know you are scheduled to visit for my birthday in the summer, but I invite you to come to Vernissia and spend the rest of these winter months here. It would please me to see you again and spend time with you.

Your Betrothed,

Aurelia

She began to fret as a month passed and he didn't come. She couldn't even soothe herself with painting, as party preparations kept her busy. Just as she sat to write him another letter, word came that he would arrive the following day. The east wing chambers were prepared for him. These weren't part of the guest manor, but in the palace itself - the same rooms he would share with Aurelia once they married.

She waited for him at the foot of the stairs leading into the courtyard. Her fingers smoothed the lapels on her warm black cloak. The carriage stopped and a footman opened the door for the prince. Aiden leapt out. She barely glimpsed his loose shirt and casual pants before he was spinning her around in a hug. She had to steady herself when he put her down.

"Ah, how I've missed you, Auri."

"You do understand it's still winter? You look ready for a summer ride through the woods."

He tossed back his shoulder-length ash brown hair and laughed. "I came to spend time with Aurelia. It is always summer where the princess of dawn resides." He gave a short bow and winked.

She grinned. "Always a charmer. Let's go inside. I'm not immune to the cold, even if you are. Promise me you'll dress warmer tomorrow."

A light dusting of snow covered the ground the next day, but the sky was clear and perfect for a walk after lunch. Aiden escorted Aurelia to the gardens. They sat at the mermaid fountain, walked under vined trellises, and talked of whatever came to mind.

"There's a reason I came late," Aiden said. "My mother is sick."

Aurelia reached out and stroked his arm. "How bad is it?"

"It's the wasting sickness. They say she only has a couple of years left to live." He sat on a bench, burying his face in his hands.

Aurelia sat behind him and put an arm around his shoulder. "I'm so sorry. If I had known, I wouldn't have expected you to come."

He dropped his hands. She could see him holding back tears. "I wanted to come. You are always surrounded by light and joy. I need that, especially now." Aiden stood, helped her up, and continued holding her hand as they walked. The path took them into the rose maze. Before long Aiden was joking and laughing as usual. "I remember the excitement of first exploring these mazes, so vast and mysterious. Now it appears so small. I yearn to see beyond Tessagonia. Once we're married I'd like to travel together, before we take the throne. The Outer Isles, perhaps even beyond, would be ours to experience."

Aurelia nodded but did not answer. She didn't understand his need to leave. Everything she loved was on this continent.

They entered the center of the maze and he grinned. "I remember the first time I came here. You rescued a crane."

The princess smiled. "That's one of my earliest memories." Her incomplete painting depicted that very crane. "I got scolded for ruining my slippers."

Aiden thought for a moment. "Do you remember what you said to me that day?"

She frowned. "No, what did I say?"

"You said, and I quote, 'Maybe next time I'll be rescuing you.' And you rescued me today, as I knew you would. Thank you... for comforting me, and for simply being here. I know I'm not Shane, but I want to be here for you as you have been for me." He embraced her and they headed back to the palace.

As the winter grew colder, they spent more time inside. They played many games of Chess and Twin Stones, and watched performances of traveling entertainers. Aurelia enjoyed her time with Aiden. He always made her laugh. But it was mostly fun, with little seriousness. She wanted to love him, but couldn't stop comparing him to his brother. She missed her discussions of literature with Shane, as Aiden didn't understand reading for pleasure. He never once inquired about her lack of painting. And there was no ember of passion when she looked in his eyes, only the spark of laughter.

The last of the snow melted on the day that Aiden departed. Aurelia kissed him on the cheek and wished him well. In return, he kissed her on both cheeks and reminded her he would be back in three months for her birthday. Watching his carriage drive off, Aurelia realized she had found a small place for him in her heart after all.

As Aurelia's eighteenth birthday neared, citizens from all throughout the kingdom came in anticipation of seeing their future queen. Tents were assembled outside the walls once lodgings became full.

The formal celebrations began as trumpets announced dawn, the time of her birth. Though it would have been acceptable for her to sleep late, Aurelia didn't want to waste a moment of her special day. She surprised the staff by joining them in the kitchen for breakfast. She talked to each one of them, starting their day with a smile. A few days before, the princess had given the cooks instructions to make hundreds of sweets. Aurelia and two of her maids each grabbed two baskets filled with these candies. Without waiting for an escort, she led them out into the city. She knew her parents would be concerned, but she wanted one last day of freedom.

For the outing she wore a simple blue dress with her hair braided into a ring atop her head. To those who hadn't seen her before, she fit right in with the handmaidens. They exited the city walls to enter the tent city. Aurelia stopped a little boy in rags and asked him to spread the word for all children to come near the gates. She gave him one of the treats and told him that every child who came to her would get one. His eyes lit up, and he ran to tell others. And they came. All morning, Aurelia and her ladies handed out candy and spoke to the young ones. They didn't know who she was, but their parents did. And as they grew older they would remember the kindness she showed that day.

Lunch was a quiet contrast. Augustus and Lorelei joined their daughter in the garden for a private picnic. Augustus joked about how long it had been since he had sat on the grass. Lorelei leaned against him and whispered something in his ear. He stopped laughing, and his face went red. The queen giggled and kissed him on the lips. Aurelia observed their affection for each other and wondered if she would be as happy with Aiden. Of course, she thought, happiness is what you make it. Joy came easily to her, so surely she would continue to find pleasure once she married.

That afternoon, King Augustus presented Aurelia to the people as their future queen. She curtsied to the crowds in respect, fully aware that a queen would be nothing without her people. Then Aiden stepped forward to be formally presented as her betrothed.

Two banquets took place simultaneously that night. Soldiers set out tables and food in the tent city, while nobility dined in the banquet hall. Entertainment at both was provided by hired performing troupes. Dancing followed dinner. Aurelia wore a violet dress the same shade as her eyes. Her hair was pulled back into a bun, with small curls left down at her temples. The betrothed couple danced alone for the first song, then the floor opened for guests to join. Aurelia didn't get much of a chance to speak with Aiden. It made her grateful they had spent the winter together. The night concluded with a magnificent show of fireworks. Aurelia felt pleased that she had done well for herself and her people.

Finally having some personal time, Aurelia spent many of the following weeks re-familiarizing herself with her other paints - watercolor, pastels, and acrylic. She tired of them after a few months. They simply didn't have the same feel as the oils. Her only time commitment didn't help, as it was regular sittings for her portrait. She coveted the artist's place on the other side of the canvas. Even the smell of the oils tempted her.

A couple weeks before the wedding, she found herself uncovering her unfinished canvas. Her last portrait session had been that morning, and she couldn't resist seeing her own work again. Most of the background was finished. An empty patch in the middle waited for her to paint the sketched crane. A woman's voice startled her.

"What a beautiful painting that is. Pity it isn't finished."

Aurelia turned to see a servant woman dusting the furniture. "I'm sorry; I didn't hear you come in. It doesn't matter in any case. I can't work on the painting just now. There are reasons it must wait."

"But you get married so soon! It would be a perfect wedding present. There's so little left to do on it, you could easily finish it in time."

Aurelia was taken aback. "A wedding present? I hadn't even thought to give one."

"This painting means so much to you. Prince Aiden would be touched if you gave it to him. And you've been so melancholy lately. A bride should be happy. I miss the joyous look that comes over your face when you paint."

Aurelia ran her hands over her satin dress as she thought for a minute, remembering her conversation with Aiden about the day she rescued the crane. He would value having a memento. And it was almost finished. She could likely complete it in a single sitting. She was so bored, and missed the feel of the oils on her brush. Surely no danger would come of it. Then it wouldn't distract her anymore. Determination filled her and she turned to the servant. "You are right. It will make a perfect wedding present. Fetch my oils and my smock."

The maid curtsied and hurried off. She returned with another servant, both carrying supplies. Aurelia slipped her arms into the smock and sat before the canvas. Once she was alone, she opened the paints. Nothing looked amiss. She sniffed them. No odd smells either. Perhaps the curse was empty after all. Smiling with confidence, she wet her brush and dabbed it in the bright red for the crane.

Her prediction that she could finish it in one sitting held true. The evening grew late, but the painting sat before her, complete. It should dry in time to frame for the wedding. Pleased with herself, she cleaned up. So much for that silly curse. She slept content that night.

"Aurelia, what have you done? Are you all right?"

Her mother's frantic voice awoke her. Aurelia sat up and blinked at her mother in the faint light coming through the window. "I'm fine. You saw the painting then?"

Lorelei frowned and knelt in front of her daughter. "You promised you wouldn't paint. Something could have happened."

"Perhaps there is no curse."

Her mother gripped her hand. "Do not scare me like that again. You have to be safe."

Aurelia sighed. "I'm sorry I worried you. But I wanted to finish the painting for Aiden as a wedding gift."

"Well, it's done now. Leave the paints be. Do not disobey me again."

The princess nodded.

A summons delayed her breakfast. The portrait artist wanted her opinion on which frame to use. Aurelia met him in the parlor. He held each frame up to the painting for her inspection. She chose the darker frame that wouldn't detract from the bright colors of her hair. After he left, she ran her fingers over the frame as it leaned against the wall. She wondered what frame she would want for the crane. A spot of color on the inside of the frame drew her eye. She rubbed it with her finger. Wet oil paint. She licked her thumb and scrubbed at the spot to clean it off. A splinter jabbed the flesh. Instinct had her yank her hand up and suck the blood off before her brain caught up to her action. A thought didn't quite form of her mother's warnings about poison as dizziness overcame her. She reached for the wall to steady herself, but collapsed as everything went dark.

Her maidservant came looking for her when she didn't return for her meal. She found Aurelia sprawled on the floor. Unable to awaken the princess, she rushed to Their Majesties' chamber. Her parents, seeing the paint on her finger, knew the curse had befallen her. Only one thing could be done. They moved her to her bedchamber, changed her into a modest sleeping gown, and cleaned her hands. Then they sent a message with their fastest courier, and waited.

When Aiden received word that Aurelia lay unconscious under a spell, he immediately confided in Shane, who offered to accompany him. Hannah, concerned for her friend, insisted on going as well. Shane tried to dissuade her as he didn't want to risk her pregnancy, now five months along. Especially with her previous miscarriage. She argued that she would worry more if she remained alone with no knowledge of Aurelia's condition. So the three departed for Vernissia.

Not willing to create more risk than necessary, the trip lasted a week. Lorelei and Augustus greeted them personally when they arrived. The queen helped an exhausted Hannah out of the carriage and escorted her to the suite she would share with Shane. Augustus took the twins directly to see the princess, worried that the extra time spent for Hannah had cut into his own daughter's time. Aurelia had not changed. Red-gold hair fanned on the pillows, pale hands lay at her sides, the flush in her cheeks and slight movement of her chest the only signs of life. One of her maidservants hovered at her side to watch for any change.

Her father sat on the edge of the bed and told the brothers how it came to pass - the curse at her unveiling, the incident with the portrait, and the promise that one could follow and bring her back to the living.

Aiden folded his hands, knuckles white. Without taking his eyes off Aurelia, he spoke to Augustus. "And as her betrothed, you sent for me. But what can I do? How am I to follow her to the spirit world?"

The king rubbed his stubbled chin. "Since Aurelia's collapse, the priest has been fasting and praying for her. It is time to interrupt his commune with the deities. Hopefully he will know what to do now."

His wife entered as he spoke. "I have also prayed to Bentos. He sent me my daughter; I am confident he will show the priest the way to bring her back. I've already asked for the priest. He is on his way."

The priest came, bringing with him the blessed rose oil. Sorrow marked his face as he looked at the princess. "I know what it is that must be done. Bentos has reminded me of others that have been sent to the spirit world. Not to commune or bring back a spirit, but to free the mind from worldly troubles. The same technique should work here." He gestured to Aiden. "Come and lie down beside her. Bentos will send you there, but you must bring yourself back. Do not lose yourself. The body can only survive for a month before the connection begins to fade. Time flows differently there. One day in the spirit realm passes as one week here. It has nearly been two weeks for Aurelia already. Seek her quickly."

Aiden stretched out on the bed and took Aurelia's nearest hand in his. "I am ready."

"Close your eyes." The priest dipped his fingers in the rose oil and pressed them to Aiden's forehead, lips, and heart. "I beseech thee, Bentos, to take this one into the spirit realm. Let his body sleep while he walks there. May Bentos watch over him during the day, and Delwyn keep him throughout the night." The onlookers watched Aiden's breathing slow until his chest barely stirred.

Aiden felt himself drift. He knew only darkness for a time. Then the world lightened. He became aware of himself standing in front of a tall, gaping steel gate. Beyond it grew a forest, faded of color. He stepped through into the shadowed woods, and the gate closed behind him. A pale sun began its descent through the ashen sky as Aiden began his search.

He saw no path, so pushed through dense foliage to create his own. Silence reigned in the spirit realm. No birds sang, no crickets chirped, he could only hear himself breaking branches and stomping down the long grass. He looked back with satisfaction to see a clear path behind him. He wouldn't lose himself in this dreary place. The sun set to be replaced by a full moon. The prince felt no hunger, but fatigue weighed him down. At last, he broke through into an empty clearing and lay down for a short rest.

The tranquil pool of water before Aurelia portrayed a full moon. Its twin in the sky showered moondust speckles, transforming her from a pale girl into something more ethereal, as if made of silver light. A white shift hung from her small, delicate frame. She had searched for a way out, stumbling through the rough forest grass, but somehow ending up at this same clearing over and over again. She knelt, leaning forward to rest her hands on the edge of the bank, entwining her fingers in the grass. Her bright hair, the only color around her, fell forward as she gazed into the crystal water. Tears filled her eyes as she considered the figure looking back at her — shining red-gold hair framing flushed skin, violet eyes sparkling, lips quirked in a smile, dressed in the red silken robe of royalty. The image of who she used to be. Aurelia reached down to the girl, yearning to be one with her again, but the water was as glass, unyielding to her touch. She sobbed, beating her fist on the surface, desperate to escape her prison. The water merely rippled without parting. Where was her prince to rescue her?

Aiden awoke to find the sun already risen. How long had he slept? He jumped up, desperate to find Aurelia and get out of this place. He looked for the trail he forged, but the path had overgrown during the night. Turning in circles, he panicked. He couldn't remember which direction he traveled, or how to get back to the gate. Picking a direction, he charged into the forest, calling out Aurelia's name.

A sound reached Aurelia. Merely a whisper on the wind. Just enough for her to lift her head. She couldn't understand the voice but knew it called to her. It was the first sound that hadn't been her own since waking in this awful place three days ago. A faint hope began to blossom and she pushed herself to her feet, wiped her swollen eyes. Her love had come to rescue her.

The next time it sounded was no clearer, but with it she saw a ripple in the leaves to her left. For the first time she wandered without returning to the mirrored pool. Guided by the murmur, the breeze, the insubstantial pull. Yet still the sun set before she found its source. And the sound was growing less frequent. She worried if she did not reach him soon, she would be lost forever.

She looked at the rising moon and knelt, raising her eyes and her hands. "Delwyn, guide me to my prince. Do not let me spend another night alone beneath your gaze."

"Aurelia…"

She clearly heard her name that time. "Shane?" She leapt to her feet. She looked around. The moonlight struck a nearby tree just right, the bark torn in the shape of an arrow. The grass looked a little clearer the way it pointed. "Thank you, Delwyn." She rushed through the thinning grass and trees. "I'm here!"

"Aurelia?!"

She broke through into another clearing, and there was Shane, waiting for her. He threw his arms around her.

His voice was hoarse, but his grip was tight. "Oh, Auri. I thought I'd never find you."

Aurelia pulled back and took a closer look. "Aiden. How… Why…"

"The priest sent me to find you. But…" He looked around. "I fear we both are lost. I don't know how to return."

Despair crushed the last of her hope. Shane wasn't coming. Her legs gave way, and she crumpled. Aiden lowered her gently to the ground, holding her shaking body close.

They fell asleep there in each other's arms, but the next morning Aurelia found herself alone again, by her familiar pond. Her loneliness and despair felt a curse worse than death.

Activities at the palace were subdued. Servants tiptoed around their king and queen. After a dinner where hosts and guests alike only nibbled at their food, Augustus asked the involved parties to meet in his sitting room. Shane helped Hannah into a velvet-lined chair and stood behind her, hands resting on the tall back of the seat. Lorelei sat next to her husband on a settee, both with shadowed eyes. Augustus took her hand as he spoke. "It's been three weeks since Aiden left. I'm afraid we may have to consider failure. Aurelia..." He cleared his throat, "Aurelia is going pale. I don't know how much longer she'll last. The priest has communed with Bentos. He said that only the power of love can guide someone through the spirit realm. If Aiden hasn't found her, then he may be lost to us as well. I'm sorry, Shane. We'll give them one more week, then send word to your parents."

Shane's fingers whitened as they dug into the chair. "Hannah, perhaps it would be best if you returned to our room. I'd like to talk to them alone." Her eyes grew worried, but she nodded and wished everyone good night, squeezing her husband's rigid arm on her way out. He took a deep breath and raised his eyes to stare at Augustus. "I think I have a way to save your daughter, and my brother as well. I can seek out Aiden with my love for him, and I love Aurelia as well. I know I can bring her back. If my love isn't strong and true enough, then no power in this world can save her."

Lorelei gasped at his revelation. Augustus slowly nodded, a mixture of pain and hope blurring his vision. "I understand why you didn't want your wife to hear that. I don't want to hurt Hannah, but for my daughter's sake I am asking you to enter the spirit realm. I pray you don't fail, for my family, for your wife, and for your brother."

The queen spoke, her voice hollow and haunting. "What shall we tell Hannah?"

Shane brought his hands up to rub his face before making his decision. "Tell her I'm going after Aiden. If all goes well, we'll all return and few will know the truth. Aurelia will marry my brother and I will return to a pleasant life with Hannah and our child." Unable to bear facing his wife, he stuck his head out the door to command a passing servant to fetch the priest.

Shane first grew aware of the washed out surroundings, then the forest beyond a steel gate. He whispered, "Bentos, lead me to my love, my Aurelia, whom you blessed with your own light." As he stepped through the gate, he caught a glimpse of color deep within the woods. A red glow flickered as fire, but he couldn't see or smell any smoke. He took in the rest of his surroundings. Nothing else stood out. He marked the direction of the pale sun before entering the forest. Letting the light beckon him, he stomped through the tall grass. The sky was only beginning to darken when he heard sobbing. A sigh of relief shuddered through him as he discovered a clearing in the woods. A girl knelt on the bank of a still pool. The red glow surrounded her, emanating from her blazing hair. He took a step toward her. "Aurelia?"

She looked up at the sound of his voice, afraid it was only an illusion. "Shane?" she whispered uncertainly.

He took three great strides to kneel at her side and pull her into his arms. "Yes, it's me. I thought I had lost you."

Bewildered, she touched his face. "But, I thought–"

"That it would be Aiden, not me? He came after you, but did not awaken. Time is running out. Everyone was afraid we'd lose you both. I volunteered to come myself." Shane pressed his cheek to her hair. "I may not be able to live with you, but I couldn't bear a world without you."

Aurelia pulled back and stood to face away from him. "I'm not the same girl here that I was there. I've lost all my gifts. I'm a klutz, my figure is bony and plain, I'm continually depressed. Can you still love me knowing I'm a façade?"

He moved in front of her and cupped her face in his hands. "You are still beautiful. You are courageous and strong. The muse didn't gift you with your love of books or your maturity. I love every bit of you." Shane ran his fingers through her thick hair. "The curse could not dim the red–gold hair that Bentos gifted you. It beckoned me; that's how I found you. My blazing princess." He placed a tender kiss on her forehead. "Aiden will be a lucky man to have you."

Moisture slipped down her cheeks. "Thank you." She took a deep breath and straightened her shoulders. "You said Aiden is still here. I found him once but we lost each other. I had hoped he had awoken. We have to find him."

"They say true love is the guide. It manifested for me in the form of flaming light. But I'm at a loss where to find my brother. Do you love him?"

"Yes. Though it's nothing compared to my feelings for you. This past winter I learned to love Aiden for who he is." She closed her eyes and pictured him. After a moment she opened her eyes and looked around. "There it is. A narrow shaft of yellow light in the distance." She smiled and grabbed Shane's hand. "Let's go."

It didn't take them long to reach him. He embraced them both, understanding immediately why Shane was there. He spoke a rough hello, his voice hoarse from shouting. Shane led them back out. They passed through the gates as the sun set and darkness engulfed them.

The queen leapt to her feet when she saw her daughter stir. As she hovered over her, she saw the brothers awaken as well. Aurelia opened her eyes and threw her arms around her mother.

"I'm sorry, Mother."

Lorelei squeezed her tight. "It's not your fault. The curse could not be prevented. But it's over now. We've had so much sorrow lately, it gladdens me to see all three of you return safely."

Shane grew cold. "What sorrow? Has something else happened?"

The king spoke from his chair near the door. "When Hannah found out what you did, she panicked. She had lost her brother-in-law and her best friend; she didn't want to lose you as well. Her body couldn't take the stress and went into labor."

Shane threw himself off the bench. "Where is she? Is she okay? What about the child? She wasn't supposed to have the baby for a few more months."

"It was too much for her. She didn't make it. The baby was too small and couldn't breathe well. He only lasted a couple of hours."

Shane's voice broke. "He? It was a boy?" He barely saw the affirming nod. His legs lost their strength and he collapsed back onto the seat, covering his face with his hands.

Aurelia covered her mouth. "Oh, Shane..."

Aiden put a hand on his brother's shoulder. "How long were we gone?"

"You were gone for nearly five weeks, Shane for four days." He cleared his throat. "We've prepared the bodies. We can send them to her homeland, or back to Arania with you."

Aiden went with his brother to make the arrangements.

That evening, Lorelei asked to speak to Aurelia and Aiden together. She looked at them as they sat on the settee without touching each other. "Aiden, after all that has happened, I have to ask. Do you love my daughter?"

He slowly shook his head. "Not enough to save her."

"What about you, Aurelia? Do you love him?"

"Yes, but it did not come naturally. I've always compared him to his brother, and only recently learned to appreciate his differences."

"So you love Shane?"

The princess smiled sadly. "I've always loved Shane, ever since we were little."

Lorelei clenched her skirt. "What grief we could have prevented if only we hadn't betrothed our young to the wrong individuals. If only we had let you choose for yourselves. I won't advise you what to do now. Your fate is in your own hands."

Epilogue

Aurelia traveled with Shane to Kether. She was his strength while he buried his wife and son. Four months later, they married. Shane gave up his place as Arania's heir, as he would someday govern Vernissia with Aurelia. Aiden followed his own heart and set sail for the Outer Isles to seek his own fate.

Bentos and Delwyn summoned the muses. The seven sisters knelt in Their presence. The Sun God's voice rumbled as he spoke to his daughters. "I hope you all followed the results of your quarrel." He looked pointedly at Enid. "I was tempted to rebuke your power, as not only did you meddle, but you threatened a life that I blessed for this world. Your mother subsided my fury. You may continue your blessings on man, but no more curses, lest you anger us again."

Delwyn smiled at her daughters. "Remember that your spheres are all equal. Even life is gladly risked by those with a higher purpose. It is not your influence that shapes man. Even we rarely interfere with their lives. They shape their own souls and destiny."

Humbled, the muses departed.

Author's Note

The Blazing Princess is my spin on Sleeping Beauty. My initial concept was off the name Aurora itself, which means dawn. Have her light tied to the sun, a literal Blazing Princess. I intended for the whole world to go dark with her. Instead, I used that imagery in a separate spirit world. I didn't like the idea of some fairy not being invited, so in my story the curse isn't due to someone being left out. Instead, it results from the muses being immortal beings, and bickering over which of them is most important. This lent well to having them all be sisters. I came up with the domain and signature color for each first, then looked up names that fit the meanings. Most of the original muse names were Welsh in origin. A couple did change later in edits.

Tesni (warmth from the sun) was initially Elisu (kind); Anwen (very beautiful); Kala (art) was initially Enfys (which means rainbow); Meinir (slender and tall); Gwynaeth (happiness); Enid (soul, life); and Carys (love).

Another name that changed was the main character, Aurora. Feedback was the name had too much Disney history and connotations. It was hard for me to imagine her with a different name, and I was attached to Aiden's nickname for her: Rory (also a nod to Gilmore Girls). But I looked up other names with similar meanings and sidestepped into Aurelia—which I think is a prettier name—and switched her nickname to Auri. Here are my initial notes!

Short story or novelette, variation on sleeping beauty. The Blazing Princess. The sun blessed her with some of its light. When she is taken from the world, everything is actually darker, like someone turned the light switch to dim. After her birth, the king and queen host a celebratory ball. Everyone is invited, including the seven muses: music, beauty, art, grace, joy, life, and love. Custom for royal born is a blessing from each muse. At the ball, the muses argue over whose gift is more important, and life decides to prove to everyone that hers trumps all. The first five give their blessings. Life gives a curse—Aurora's life will end at age sixteen. Love counters death with her blessing, that the girl will only be banished to the other realm. Her body will sleep, but her soul will be gone. True love will be able to reach her and bring her back to the realm of the living.

Another aspect of the original tales I don't like is that our princess gets kissed by some stranger. Even in the Disney version, Aurora only gets a few brief meetings with the prince, and is supposed to get woken by True Love's kiss? Instead, I used the idea of love saving her as an opportunity for her parents to get involved and try to save her, betrothing her to someone she could grow up knowing and hopefully fall in love with. But my extra twist was having her fall for the wrong prince.

Mirror

Mary W. Jensen

Contents

1

Lady Sophia wandered through Market Square, hardly noticing the sweaty smells of the commoners or the raised voices calling their wares or haggling with customers. She usually sent her servants to shop for her, but on this day, she needed a distraction. A cart driver swerved when she didn't move out of his path. His swearing didn't penetrate her heavy thoughts. One month to the day had passed since her husband had set sail. She longed to see him. The manor had been so empty without his laughter. He hadn't even told her where he was going or when he would return. Only that the sea was calling for him once more.

She didn't understand how he could leave her. He had always praised her beauty; in fact, considered her the most beautiful lady in the land. She placed a hand on her slightly swollen stomach. Had he found her pregnant form ungainly? Sophia sighed and lifted a swath of cloth from the booth in front of her. The indigo should hide her condition a bit longer. The merchant agreed to send a bolt of the fabric to the Lady's personal dressmaker for no extra charge. She sauntered toward a display of jewelry in a lighter mood. She heard a desperate yell coming from the direction of her parked carriage and had to take her eyes off the goal. What could possibly be wrong?

Her steward caught up to her. "Madame, a letter has come. They saw your carriage, so gave it to me rather than send it to the manor."

Sophia's breathing faltered. Could it be word that his ship had reached port? "Read it to me."

He broke the seal. "Lady Sophia, we regret to inform you that The Dark Lady has been found drifting out at sea. The cargo is missing and the crew, including your husband, is dead." The steward cleared his throat and bowed his head. "I'm sorry, Madame. Truly sorry."

Despair crippled her for a moment and she felt the steward grab her arm as her vision blurred. What would she do without him? Why, why did he ever have to leave? Anger rushed in, strengthening her. She straightened her shoulder, shook off the steward's hand. Father had been right; she never should have let herself be wooed by a common sailor. He got her with child and left her to deal with his burden alone. At least Father had left everything to her. She didn't need a man.

A glint of gold caught her eye. A merchant from the Outer Isles had his wares set across the way. His dark hands polished a mirror with an elaborate gilded wood frame. He turned it and stepped aside, so all Sophia saw was her own reflection. One couldn't tell she was pregnant. She flushed, pleased at her still apparent beauty, and that no tears had tarnished it. She had to have the mirror. The only ones in the manor were small or handheld. This full-length one would do justice to her glory. She paid extra to have men deliver the mirror to Redcap Manor, a half-day's travel outside the city.

Sophia had them set the mirror across from her bed, then sent everyone out. This was a mirror to be left alone with. She needed to see her beauty. But that wasn't enough. She needed to know she remained the most beautiful woman in the land, though no one remained to tell her. Except the servants, of course, but who knew if they'd be telling the truth or merely trying to please. With a sigh, she ran a finger across her reflection's lips. "Mirror, mirror, I demand, who is the fairest in the land?" A chill rushed through her finger, up her arm, and into her heart. Her image swirled in the mirror to be replaced by that of a cloaked figure. The lilting voice that emerged banished any fear that might have existed.

"Lady Sophia, thou art truly the fairest in the land."

Sophia's eyes glinted with delight. "A magic mirror! I knew you were special. How do I know you are not simply telling me what I wish to hear?"

"I see all. I know all. I cannot tell a lie."

"Cast back your hood, mirrored one. I foresee myself spending much time in front of this mirror, and I'd like to know who is gazing back at me."

Dark hands reached up to push back the hood to reveal a young woman from the Outer Isles with their brown skin and black curls. Her face was round and boring. Certainly no competition for Sophia's sunlit hair, pale beauty, regal cheekbones, and perfectly formed, rose-tinted lips. She smiled, pleased by the contrast. "And you will come whenever I call?"

"I am always here, and shall show myself at your request. Such is my fate. My name is-"

Sophia waved a hand in dismissal. "I care not what your given name is. You are Mirror, that is all. Now go, so I may bask in my beauty once more."

As her pregnancy continued, Lady Sophia's temper grew along with her belly. She snapped at the servants, refused to see visitors, and cursed the babe for driving away her husband. She made it no secret that she held no love for the child. The steward, aware of her lack of regard, took it upon himself to arrange for a nursemaid who could care for the child. Sophia spent most of her day locked in her bedchamber. Every evening she would beseech the mirror, finding comfort in the fact that her beauty did not fade despite her ungainly walk. In fact, Mirror told her that the fertile belly made her even more envied among the women of court.

When the babe came, labor was long and hard. The midwife at last announced the birth of a baby girl. Lady Sophia refused to see the baby, or to acknowledge it with a name. The birthing weakened her, leaving her bedridden for three days. She cried as she could not stand before the mirror for the first time in the five months since its purchase. Meanwhile, the nursemaid fed and cared for the little girl. The servants nicknamed her Snow for her pale white skin. One month later, the steward found Sophia in good enough strength and disposition for him to sway her to name the child.

Korina had her mother's blue eyes and her father's black hair. As she grew, she saw only glimpses of her mother. She lived in a separate wing of the manor, ate in the kitchen with the servants, and loved her nursemaid, Anna, as a mother. The girl admired Lady Sophia, but did not have a personal connection to her. For her part, Sophia preferred to exist as if she didn't have a child. She returned to mingle with the other ladies at court and held elaborate parties at the manor. Each night she reveled in the Mirror's unchanging message: no one could surpass her beauty.

But Korina grew in beauty and curiosity. By age seven, she had the manor explored, as well as the gardens. All except the chambers of Lady Sophia, of course. Those doors remained locked at all times, and even Korina could not find a secret entrance. She satisfied herself instead by listening to her mother's voice through the door. She couldn't understand what was said, and knew not why her mother spoke aloud when only she was in the room, but enjoyed the sing-song tone she heard before scampering off to bed.

It was the night of Korina's twelfth birthday that everything changed for the lady of the house. Oblivious to the fact that the servants were hosting a birthday party for the girl, Lady Sophia kept to her usual routine. After dinner with a few guests, she retired to her bedchamber. She changed into a red silk nightdress and drank a glass of red wine as she stood before her mirror. "Mirror, mirror, I demand, who is the fairest in the land?" On other nights, she would hear about her beauty, then speak with Mirror for a while, inquiring what else she had seen—any news Sophia could use at court, or bargains to be made in business. She waited for Mirror's response this night.

"Lady Sophia, it is true that few come close to the intensity of your beauty, but there is one more fair than thee."

Sophia gasped and the glass she held slipped out of her hands. Red wine spread away from her feet to stain the ivory carpet.

"Mirror, I command you to show me who could possibly be more beautiful than your Mistress."

The image of the cloaked woman swirled to be replaced by that of a young girl, with pale skin, blue eyes, and long black hair.

Lady Sophia dug her nails into her palms. "Who is this girl? Tell me!"

Once again, the image changed to Mirror's cloaked form. "Do you not recognize your own daughter?"

Only one of her own blood could ever reach nigh her own status. But what was she to do? She couldn't have her own brat knock her off her pedestal. Nor could she hide the girl in the manor house forever. An idea came to her, and she smirked. "Mirror, who of my staff is most loyal to me?"

This time the image of a man appeared, red hair and bearded, with piercing gray eyes, before showing Mirror once more. "He who supplies meat for your table. Rolan the Hunter."

"Mmm. How very fitting. He shall carry out my plan."

First thing the next morning, Lady Sophia sent a discreet message to Rolan, asking the hunter to meet her in the garden at midnight. He came as she asked and knelt before his lady.

"I have a task for you, Hunter. But you must swear that only you and I shall know of it."

"On my life do I swear, milady."

"Then arise and listen closely. There is a threat to my well-being that must be dealt with."

Rolan's eyes hardened. "Who dares to threaten thee?"

Sophia's voice dropped to a whisper. "My own daughter."

His brow furrowed in confusion. "Korina? Are you positive?"

She snapped with irritation, "Of course I'm positive. But who else would believe me? Many of the servants are already under her spell. I need you to draw her into the forest and dispose of her. We can attribute her death to a hunting accident."

The hunter bowed his head. "I did not mean for you to doubt my loyalty. I shall obey."

"Good. Each night I shall wait here until you have something to report. And I expect results within one week. If you do not follow through, I'll name you a traitor and it will mean your death."

He nodded and turned on his heel to leave her presence.

That weekend, Rolan invited Korina on her first hunt. The girl fidgeted as Anna braided her hair. The idea of a hunt didn't excite her, but the opportunity to go outside the walls thrilled her. Once in the courtyard, the hunter lifted the girl onto the back of a calm-natured mare and leapt onto his own steed. Rolan commented on how tense she sat.

"Haven't you ridden a horse before?"

She blushed. "A stable boy showed me the basics, but I've only been able to ride around the paddock."

He promised to go slow, and they headed out the gates. The guards, Meric and Janisen, waved as they passed. Once deep within the cover of the forest, Rolan dismounted and helped her do the same. He signaled for her to be quiet and follow him.

They followed a worn path deeper into the foliage. It led to a stream where a boar drank from the clear water. Rolan cupped a hand to Korina's ear and brought his mouth close to whisper for her to circle to the animal's left while he went right. Then she could startle it toward him. She nodded in understanding and moved as he instructed. At his signal, she waved and shouted at the boar. Instead of heading for the hunter, it turned and charged for the girl. Korina yelped, turned to run, and stumbled, catching her fall with her hands. She held her breath as the boar ran by. A whistling sound cut through the air and Korina felt a sharp pain in her left shoulder. She grasped where it hurt, and her fingers came away sticky with blood. She looked around to see a dagger stuck in the ground nearby and the boar was nowhere in sight.

Furious, Korina turned to the hunter. "You missed the boar and grazed my arm!"

His face was grim. "Usually I don't miss my mark. I'm sorry I missed." He moved past her to pick up the dagger. Suddenly, he whirled around and lunged for her with his left hand, dagger poised in his right.

Korina jumped backward, but his fingers caught some of her hair, yanking it out of her head. She screamed and fled through the river and into the trees on the other side. The hunter sprinted after her. The woods suddenly broke before her and the girl skidded to a stop at the edge of a cliff.

The hunter threw his dagger, this time making its mark. It pierced Korina's back, knocking her forward. She fell thirty feet to the ground below. Rolan looked down at her unmoving form and nodded in satisfaction. He took the lock of hair still gripped in his fist, and returned to the manor.

The hunter told everyone that Korina had run ahead and fallen off a cliff to her death, her body irretrievable. The household mourned. At midnight, he presented the girl's torn hair to Lady Sophia. Not satisfied, she returned to inquire of Mirror. When she was shown Korina's body lying at the bottom of the cliff, dagger in her back, she at last smiled in satisfaction.

L ady Sophia's land lay on the edge of Arania, near to the Sea of Mystery, the great enchanted lake in the center of the continent of Tessagonia. Four kingdoms border the inland sea, but a fifth kingdom floats above it: Lesenti, realm of the seven muses. It happens that the day after Korina's "accident", one muse took a leisurely flight over the land. Tesni spotted the motionless body below and dipped her green pegasus down to look. The muse of compassion felt life beating faintly within the girl. Gently, she lifted the child onto her steed and they flew back to the realm above. She and her sisters nursed the girl back to health, using their powers of blessing along with the enchanted water from the sea below.

Korina didn't waken for a full week. Once she did, her surroundings amazed her. She lay in a room with walls and floor of crystal. The chamber was filled with the bed that she lay in, an enormous dresser, a desk and a chair, all of a dark timber intricately fashioned with representations of the sun and the moon. Wanting to get a closer look, she sat up and tried to stand. Her legs failed her, and she collapsed back onto the bed. Feeling helpless, she buried herself under the golden weaved quilt to slip back into sleep.

A clank of stoneware awoke her. She peeked out to see a woman setting a tray with food and drink onto the desk, her back to Korina. A golden braid fell to her waist over loose flowing yellow robes that prompted thoughts of daffodils and playing in the sunlight. The woman turned, a youthful smile on her face.

"'Tis good to see you awake. I am sure my sisters will be joyous as well to hear the news."

"Where am I? How long have I been here?"

"My sister Tesni brought you here to Lesenti one week past." She sat on the bed, putting her hand over the girl's. "You were near death. We nursed you back to health."

"Did you say we're in Lesenti? And Tesni, that's the name of one of the seven muses... Does that mean I'm in the realm of the muses?"

The woman laughed, the sound like tinkling bells. "Yes, you are. This room is one of the guest rooms of the Diamond Castle."

"Then if Tesni is your sister, you must be a muse as well."

"Of course. I should have introduced myself earlier. I am Gwynaeth. Or Gwyn, if you like. What is your name?"

"Korina."

"What a beautiful name for a beautiful girl."

Another woman entered the open doorway. She wore silver robes, her earthy brown hair pulled into a bun. Gwyn introduced Enid to Korina.

Enid pulled the chair next to the bed and sat in front of the two. "Do you remember what happened before we found you?"

The girl nodded. "Rolan took me hunting. But instead of hunting boar as I thought, he tried to kill me." She shuddered. "When I felt that knife in my back, and began to fall, I thought he'd succeeded. Everything went black. I don't even remember hitting the ground." She sat up, ignoring the blood rush from her head. "Surely someone must be looking for me. The steward, my nurse, any of the staff."

Gwyn ran her hands over Korina's midnight hair. "We've observed the place we found you, and the surrounding woods, but have seen no one. I'm sorry."

Enid nodded. "The hunter must have told them you were dead. There's plenty of room here if you'd like to stay with us."

Korina pulled her knees to her aching chest. Didn't anyone care enough to send a search party? Mother would have allowed for time off for a few of the guards to search the forest. Wouldn't she? Maybe... maybe no one cared to look after all. She had never heard of anyone ever visiting Lesenti, and here they were offering to let her stay. She let their warmth and her own curiosity fill the void that had opened inside her. "I'd like to stay. Thank you."

The sisters advised her to eat slowly and sleep as oft as she needed. She followed their instructions to the letter, wanting to recover as quickly as possible. A whole realm awaited her exploration. A few days later, Meinir helped her exercise her legs by giving a tour of the castle.

Spacious rooms filled with treasures and furnishings, in styles Korina had never seen, were introduced as the chambers of Bentos and Delwyn Themselves, for their visits. She gaped at the thought of sharing the same roof with the Sun God and Moon Goddess. Other rooms similar to her own were reserved for visitors and those who served the deities.

"But how do you get visitors here? No one else has pegasi to fly them."

"There are secret ways. Bentos and Delwyn have the power to open portals to the chosen few. We sisters also have the opportunity to bring visitors. A pegasus is strong enough to carry two passengers, but we also have a carriage. Though that requires harnessing four pegasi, so we all have to agree on the matter."

By the end of another week, Korina felt well enough to venture outside. As the large diamond door opened in front of her, she gasped with delight. Sunlight reflected off a crystal landscape on the clouds. Seven more buildings spread across its surface, each assembled from precious gems. The dwellings of the muses, each built in their signature colors. A dome of emeralds, an elaborate palace made of the delicate pink kunzite, an amethyst pagoda, a spiral tower of turquoise, a golden topaz pyramid, a moonstone keep, and dual towers of ruby connected by arches.

The muses had never spent so much time with one so young. They enjoyed her pleasure as she discovered their world. Each took a turn hosting her for three months, sharing their time and gifts.

Tesni, muse of compassion, frequently went to the mainland and returned with injured birds or other small creatures. She kept them in the flourishing jungle of the center room of her dome. Korina learned how to care for them and bring them back to health.

Anwen, muse of beauty, dressed her in long gorgeous gowns and spent many nights combing the girl's hair while they talked of the beauty in the universe—stars glistening in the sky, the curves of a swan, silk draped over a well-formed figure, the rainbows created when the sun bounced off the crystal surrounding her palace.

Kala, muse of art, taught Korina about the cultures of lands far from Tessagonia, showing her the history and value of each different sculpture, chair, and painting in her pagoda. Some she collected from her travels and others made with her own skill. The girl took an interest in pottery. She loved the feel of the clay spinning and molding beneath her hands.

Korina learned to dance on the top of Meinir's tower. She didn't care for the partnered routines the muse of elegance taught her, but spent a lot of time perfecting the lively step dances. The quick steps made a ringing music that echoed through the turquoise stone.

Gwynaeth, muse of joy, shared the ecstasy of flight, up through the clouds on her pegasus. Korina whooped with delight as the wind whipped through her hair. From above, Lesenti looked like a geode broken open and framed with cotton. She never wanted to leave.

Her time with Enid contrasted with the rest. The muse of life had a more serious demeanor. Korina did not play or learn any new skills. Enid sat her down in the keep's library and explained the importance of life and wisdom. What if a muse hadn't found her at the bottom of that cliff? She would be dead. Korina wanted to have fun and enjoy life, but Enid's words echoed in the back of her mind as she explored the keep.

Carys, muse of love, told tales of heroism and romance. The only boys Korina knew were those that worked at the manor. They were nice, but nothing special. She didn't understand this concept of love that the muse told her of. Lady Sophia seemed to do well enough alone. She needed no man. Thinking of her mother led her to wonder if she cared for Korina. The girl knew her mother did not love her, but didn't know what life would be like otherwise. Perhaps that's what Enid meant. Here, Korina had friends in the muses. She couldn't imagine being truly alone. She wondered if perhaps her mother was lonely after all. If only they spent time together, would Lady Sophia love her? After nearly two years with the muses, she considered the possibility of going home. Surely her mother would be glad to see her alive. They could start over, form a new relationship.

Korina began the walk from Carys' towers to Gwyn's pyramid. She wanted to ask Gwyn to fly her back to the mainland. A cramp in her stomach cut through her thoughts and she felt a wetness trickle down her leg. Her cry echoed over the crystal. Enid came running out of the nearby keep.

"What's wrong, Korina?"

"I don't know. I hurt. And I think I'm bleeding."

Enid sighed with relief. "You'll be fine. You are finally a woman. Come inside and I'll explain. This is a very important part of life."

About one week later, once Korina felt clean again, she resumed her purpose. Gwyn agreed to fly her down, but refused to take her to the manor.

"Someone there wants you dead. Wait until we know it's safe. We'll fly down tonight, but only to look. It would be detrimental for you to return to a place that could bring you harm and un-happiness."

Back in the manor on the land below, Lady Sophia continued her nightly demand of Mirror. But Lesenti was the one place where Mirror's powers could not reach. Thus, her answer stayed consistent, "Thou art the fairest in the land." But the night Korina flew down to see the manor, Mirror betrayed the girl. "Your daughter lives. She came out of the clouds on a pegasus with one of the muses."

The revelation shocked Lady Sophia. "You told me she was dead. If you cannot see into Lesenti, then you are not as powerful as I thought. I will have to deal with her myself. No one else can be trusted. That includes you. You have proven useless to me." She opened a chest and removed a large black piece of fabric, intending to cover the mirror.

"Wait! I have a solution more assured than death."

Intrigued, Sophia set the fabric aside. "What does this solution entail?"

"There is a spell that will trap her in this mirror. The same spell that captured me."

Sophia furrowed her brow. "How would you gain from this?"

"I gain my freedom if another takes my place. You've said so yourself: she is your only competition. Once she is out of the way, you will have no use for me or this mirror. We'll both be happy, with no blood on anyone's hands."

"How do I know she won't work a deal for her escape as you are attempting for yourself?"

"Sell the mirror with her trapped within. She will not know the spell, so will have no way to coerce someone to free her."

The lady smiled. "Trapped forever in a mirror for her insolence. I am fond of the idea." She draped herself across her bed. "Now tell me how this spell is done."

The scouting proved useful, but disappointing. The hunter still resided at the manor. It would be too risky to return if his motives remained the same. Korina didn't know why he wanted her dead, but didn't really want to find out. She sulked to the muses, reassuring them she enjoyed her stay but wanted to return home. Enid came up with the solution.

"For you to exist in that world, the hunter must not. I shall visit him tomorrow night and curse him with the fate he meant to deal to you."

Korina caught her breath. "You mean to kill him?"

"He does not deserve of the gift of life."

The girl frowned and looked to the other sisters for support.

Carys took her hand. "How badly do you want to go home?"

Korina remembered stories of criminals taken before the king. Attempted murderers were put to death as surely as the successful ones. In her case, there would be no proof, merely a young girl's word against a seasoned hunter. She nodded slowly. "I understand. I won't let him keep me from living the life I should."

Lady Sophia woke restless the next morning. She wanted to prepare the spell, but didn't have all the ingredients. With the market closed for the day of meditation, she would have to wait until the morrow. One item could be procured, however. She sent for the hunter once more. He came to her as she ate her lunch of quail.

"M'lady, how may I serve you?"

She tore off a piece of bird flesh and fondled the stripped bone. "Do you save the skulls of the creatures you hunt?"

Rolan's eyes flicked to the quail. He furrowed his brow. "At times, but only of the larger prey."

"But I require a smaller skull that might fit in my palm." She pouted and curled her fingers around the bone.

The hunter knew better than to question his mistress. "I can do as you ask, but it takes time to clean a skull. How soon do you need it?"

She sighed at the thought of waiting longer. "I'll give you three days."

He bowed. "It will be done."

The first day of waiting, Sophia sent a servant to the market with her shopping list: a glass bowl, seeds of the cusklo flower, and a rock of sea salt. The servant returned with all but the seeds. Cusklo was native to the Outer Isles, and none of the locals carried it. However, the servant also reported hearing rumors of one of their ships being docked on the coast. Sophia could wait for merchants to travel inland as they had before, but instead sent a courier out to the coast to get some directly.

After the three days, Sophia waited for Rolan to seek her out. As the day wore on, she grew terse. The staff cringed and attempted to stay out of her way. She paced the dining room as a maid scurried over with her dinner platter. The girl placed it on the table and began her retreat. Lady Sophia glanced at the plate—bread, noodles in a white sauce, and baked apple slices. She scowled. "Where's the meat?"

The maid jumped and spun back toward her mistress, keeping her head down. "Rolan hasn't brought game for three days now. No one has seen him."

"Why hasn't this been reported to me?"

"You were the last to see him. We assumed you sent him some-where."

"I gave him a task, but that shouldn't have interfered with his duties. Send someone to his lodgings at once."

"Yes'm." The maid curtsied and hurried out of the room.

Sophia swept the plate off the table and felt some satisfaction as it crashed on the floor, breaking in half. Had the hunter failed her again? If he fled, she would seek him out and kill him. She soon learned that wouldn't be necessary. The maid returned with the news that they found Rolan the Hunter dead in his room, no wounds or signs of the cause of death.

Sorrow overcame her for a moment. Rolan, her only confidante, and most loyal servant, was gone. But she had more important things to do than mourn. She straightened her shoulders. "I had tasked him with cleaning an animal skull for me. Was there one in the room?"

"Yes, there was one soaking."

"Is there anyone who can finish the process?"

The maid gave a one shoulder shrug. "The cook may."

"Make sure it happens or go to town yourself and hire someone to get it done."

"Yes'm."

With the judgment complete, Enid let Korina know she could return home. Having spent so long with the sisters, Korina stayed one more day with each muse to say a proper goodbye. After the week of being lavished with gifts, and assured that she would be welcome back if things didn't go well, the young woman flew down to the woods on the yellow pegasus. She whispered goodbye to Gwynaeth's mount and walked to the edge of the forest. The guards hadn't yet opened the manor gates for the morning. Korina carefully smoothed her long black hair and straightened the rose gown Anwen had given her. Taking a deep breath, she picked up her bundle of belongings and left the shadows of the trees.

"Meric, Janisen, open up." She rattled the gate.

A burly man came into view. Korina grinned as she saw his ashen hair still stood up in every direction. He narrowed his eyes as he looked her up and down. "Who're you? What's yer business this time of mornin'?"

She did a twirl. "Janisen, it's me. Korina."

His eyes grew wide, and his face lost some of its wrinkles. "Our little Snow is alive? Bless the Gods, girl. Come in!" The keys clanged against the metal as he fumbled in his hurry to unlock the gate. Once the bars were out of his way, he pulled her up for a tight hug. "It's been two long years. You're as beautiful as ever. What happened ta you?"

"I've been in Lesenti, living with the muses."

His eyes bugged again, and his jaw dropped so he looked like a fish out of water. "Everyone will be excited ta hear yer tale. Git along and tell the rest of the folk. You can fill me an' Meric in tonight." He winked and waved her toward the manor.

Her reunion with the rest of the staff went much the same way. Before long, most of the household had gathered in the parlour to celebrate her life and hear her tale. Korina glowed with every-one's joy at her return, but her stomach twisted as she wondered what her mother's reaction would be. She perked up as she heard her mother speak to the steward outside the door.

"What is all this commotion about? Why isn't my breakfast ready?"

"Madame, there is a very important someone here who is waiting to see you."

"Then it is a splendid thing I don't eat in my bathrobes. Don't keep them waiting. Let me in immediately."

Korina stood up from the settee as the door opened. She watched as shock crossed her mother's face before becoming the epitome of composure. Lady Sophia crossed the room to embrace her. "We thought you dead. Welcome home, daughter."

The muses watched their charge's reunion with her mother. Korina seemed to be in safe and loving hands, so they let her be to live her life anew.

Lady Sophia didn't let Korina out of her sight. She allowed the girl to eat by her side, educated her in the ways of court, and let her choose Sophia's dress for the party she was to host in two days. She praised her daughter about the gowns from Anwen and patiently listened to her tales of the last two years. They only had a few minutes away from each other that day, as Sophia attended to a package that had come in.

The staff wondered at the change in their mistress, who had never so much as acknowledged her daughter. But they kept their speculations to themselves so as not to dishearten Korina. The young woman glowed at her mother's attention.

Korina trembled with pleasure when Sophia invited her to her chambers that night. Her eyes watered as she examined her mother's room, refusing to blink, afraid it would disappear. A full-length mirror stood across from the bed; a woven mat depicting roses covered the lush ivory carpet at its foot. All the furniture had golden engravings and knobs. Only the rooms of the Diamond Castle rivaled this one in elegance. Korina ran a finger over the red silk quilt on the enormous bed. She glanced at Sophia, who gestured for her to sit down. She sank into the mattress, so much softer than the one in her own room. Her mother took a brush from one of the vanity's many drawers and sat on the bed beside her.

"Would you brush my hair, Korina?"

The young woman took the offered brush. She willed her hands steady as she let the pins out of Sophia's hair and brushed the waist-length locks. "You're so beautiful, Mother."

"As are you, my child."

Korina blushed at the compliment.

"Stay with me tonight. I'll inform the staff so that no one will worry."

She jerked with surprise and inwardly berated herself as the brush yanked the hair with her movement, creating a tangled knot. She gently worked it out and forced her heart rate back down. "I can go fetch my things. If you really mean it, that is."

Sophia turned to take the brush and place a reassuring hand on her daughter's shoulder. Her voice crooned. "Of course I mean it. I regret all those years of dismissing you. I didn't truly value your presence until you were gone. You look so much like your father. I lost him, but the Gods gave you back to me. Now that I have you back, I want to make up for lost time. No need to get your things. You can sleep in your chemise."

Korina nodded eagerly. Lady Sophia helped her undress before donning her own nightgown.

"There's something I want to show you."

Korina couldn't imagine how the day could get any better. Sophia put her hand on her shoulder and guided her to the mirror. Her mother stood behind her, a head taller than the girl. The mother put her hands on her daughter's shoulders and looked straight into the mirror.

"Now watch. Mirror, mirror, I demand, who is the fairest in the land?"

Korina's eyes widened as the mirror changed; a swirling mist coalesced into the figure of a dark-skinned woman.

"Only one surpasses your own beauty. The Lady Korina who stands before you."

The girl's breath stuck in her throat. Lady? Her, the most beautiful in all the land? A squeeze on her shoulders reminded her to breathe, but words remained lost to her.

"Speak to the mirror, child. Ask it anything you please. It will not lie."

Korina hesitated before speaking. "Tell me of my father. Sophia says I look like him, but I know nothing of him."

While Mirror spoke of a dark-haired young sailor smitten for a lady from a rich house, Lady Sophia set a tripod table beside the girl, then opened the chest in the back corner of the room where she stored the items she would need. She centered the glass bowl on the table, set the quail skull and rock of sea salt inside, then scattered the delicate lacey pods of the cusklo seeds over both. After glancing to make sure Korina still gazed at the mirror, she took a sharpened letter opener from her vanity and held her wrist over the bowl.

Lady Sophia drew the letter opener across the tender skin of her wrist until blood painted the skull. As the seeds and salt soaked up her life-force, she murmured the words given to her. "Mahallaliel, Kabarac, Great Ones of the Outer Isles, take the one before the glass, preserve them for all time, unless another is given; Shamanuc, Velekai, let it be done."

Korina frowned as the dark woman stopped mid-story. She opened her mouth to protest, but the woman in the mirror put her hands up to the other side of the glass. All thoughts left her head as a force compelled her to place her hands over the other's. She gasped as her palms met flesh, then cried out as the mist of darkness enfolded the room. The human touch on her hands disappeared, and she felt only glass. The mist cleared enough for her to see. She still stood before the mirror, but on the wrong side. The dark woman stood next to Lady Sophia in the bedroom. She pushed the mirror's surface, but nothing happened. Her hands traveled over the entire surface, but it remained solid. Her eyes darted around her. Only a dark mist filled her vision. She looked back as her mother spoke.

"Mirror, mirror, I demand, who is the fairest in the land?"

The words spilled out of Korina. "Thou art the most fair in the land."

"And do you tell the truth, Mirror?" Sophia's face twisted scorn on the last word.

Tears streamed down Korina's cheeks, but words forced themselves out of her mouth once more. "I see all. I know all. I cannot tell a lie."

"Very good. You are dismissed. Forever."

The mirror went black. Korina sank to her knees, helpless. Her thoughts drifted to the incident with the hunter, and she wondered why fate held such contempt for her. The mirror lightened, catching her eye, and she understood what was meant by seeing all. The scene played before her of Rolan meeting with Lady Sophia, and her heart broke as she heard her own mother sentence her to death. Why had she returned to the manor? She should have stayed with the muses. Their company was much preferred to this bleakness.

3

K orina learned to use the mirror to see the world she longed to be part of. She saw Lady Sophia hire a courier to give the mirror back to the Islanders, looked out over the long voyage to the Outer Isles, and could do nothing as the mirror was stuffed into a warehouse with other traded goods. Her friends at Lesenti were blocked to her, so she turned her view elsewhere. She remembered Sophia's talk of court and realized that she could finally see it herself. The ladies and their entourages kept Korina entertained for a few years, but her all-seeing view took away any intrigue and mystery it might have held. She learned Arania had two princes, but the adolescent princes were gossiped of more than seen. She turned to the other kingdoms to see if they were more interesting. Kether and Senatin bored her, so she moved on to the fourth kingdom, Vernissia. Finally, a story caught her interest. The princess had just turned eighteen and her betrothed, one of Arania's own princes, presented to the people.

Korina spied on the prince as he visited his princess, hoping to see the wondrous love Carys had told her about. Her heart sank as her true vision saw no romance, only friendship between the two. Was there no such thing as love in this world? Her heart went out to this prince, fated to marry without love. He engulfed her vision, and she lost all desire to look elsewhere. She admired his strong face, long ashen hair, and playful nature. How could the princess not love such a noble man? When she heard his name, she engraved it upon her heart. Aiden.

She cried with him as the princess fell under a spell. Even knowing he could not hear her, she called out to him when he entered the spirit realm on a futile mission to rescue his betrothed. Korina feared for Aiden. What if he became trapped in the spirit realm as she was trapped here? She watched in awe as the prince's twin brother risked his own world to save the princess, all for love. So true love did exist. But not for her. Still trapped in a mirror, forgotten in a warehouse, growing older but not truly aging. Why bother desiring that which she could never have? She caressed Aiden's image in the mirror as he woke from his enchanted slumber and wished him well. The mirror went dark as she curled up and let the nothingness surround her.

A strong male voice brought Korina to instant awareness. "Mirror, if you could speak, what stories would you have to tell?" The words echoed around her as the mirror swirled and cleared. She stood to face it, crossing her arms in front of her, shamed that she wore only a too-small chemise. Though she knew his question was rhetorical, the mirror's power compelled her to answer. "Tales of subterfuge and betrayal. Of longing and loneliness..." As she spoke, the room beyond the glass fully came into focus. She would have gasped if words didn't continue to spill from her mouth. There, on the other side of the mirror, within arm's reach but so very far away, stood none other than Prince Aiden. His shocked expression mirrored her own emotion. Her gaze took him in. He had changed in the time she slept; eyes more serious, a rough stubble on his chin.

"... This mirror has changed hands numerous times. So many souls have seen themselves in this mirror, but few have seen within it." Once the ambiguous answer finally rattled to an end, she swallowed to moisten her dry throat. She hesitated to open her mouth again, unsure if the words to emerge would be her own. He spoke before she found her own words.

"Who are you? What magic is this?"

A weight lifted from her vocal cords. Perhaps she had more freedom with her answer as he directed this question to her, not the mirror. "My name is Korina. I know not the magic that powers this mirror, only that I am trapped here and must answer truth for any questions asked." She told him how her own mother betrayed her and conspired to entrap her.

Aiden frowned. "Who is this woman who treats her own daughter this way? Where can I find her?"

"My mother is Lady Sophia of Redcap Manor, just outside the forest at the inner border of Arania." She watched his fists curl and posture stiffen.

His voice dropped to a quiet but deadly tone. "I will not permit such actions within my own borders. It is time to return home."

Her blood rushed as his gaze softened.

"I came to the Outer Isles to find a purpose. You've given me something worth fighting for." He pressed his palm to the mirror. "Do you know how to break this spell?"

Korina looked away. The hopelessness returned to clench her heart in its fist. "I did not hear the spell, and the mirror blocks me from seeing."

"I promise to find a way to free you."

His words held no consolation for her. "I saw you with Aurelia. I know you will do everything in your power to seek my freedom. Your heart is noble. But all you can do may not be enough."

She refused to see his face, but heard the pain in his voice. "So you already know of my failure. It changes nothing. I will not fail this time. I'll take the next ship home to the mainland and will speak to you then."

She felt his presence leave and only looked up when the mirror had already darkened.

Shamed by the way she treated the only one to help her, Korina put her back to the mirror and scanned the surrounding mist. How could she distract herself until Aiden's return? She took a single step into the shifting darkness. It had a solid feel to it. She brought her hands together and the mist between her palms coalesced into a ball. It reminded her of the clay Kala taught her to shape. A smile flitted as her fingers moved over the dark ball. No more would Korina sleep away her confinement.

After what seemed like an eternity, but was in truth only a single day, Korina saw Aiden again. The view behind him had changed from the crowded warehouse to a large cabin on a ship. Fit for a prince. Korina's gaze caught on the view of the wild, free ocean outside the window. She wondered what the ocean smelled like. The mirror's power showed many things, but she missed the smell of trees and fresh baked bread... the feel of a warm quilt, a bath... the cool taste of water...

Aiden interrupted her musing. "We're on our way home. I was lucky to catch a ship going the right direction." He looked past her. "What are those objects behind you? I don't remember seeing anything there."

Korina picked up a smoky vase and showed it to him. "I've found I can do pottery to pass the time."

His eyebrows rose. "I've never met a noblewoman that knew pottery."

She laughed. "Well, I'm not your typical noblewoman. All I know of court is what I've seen from this side of the mirror."

"Aurelia would paint. I respect the arts, but I prefer to spend my free time playing strategy games like Twin Stones."

"About Aurelia... I'm sorry for what I said before. I did not mean to offend you."

He sighed and sat on the canopy bed, half turned away from her. "I would have married Aurelia, you know. I do love her... but not as my brother does. After we returned from the spirit world, Shane was free to marry her. I had always wanted to travel, but was obligated in my princely duties and in the betrothal to Aurelia. But after everything that happened, no one held me back when I decided to leave. These past two years I've been sailing, visiting lands even beyond the Outer Isles. Such wondrous diversity. I've been collecting souvenirs, artifacts that hold many stories within them."

"How did you find this mirror?"

Aiden looked toward the mirror, but his eyes did not focus on her. "I was island hopping through the Outer Isles, delaying my return voyage. I heard some native Islander sailors speaking of the mirror. Rumor said that someone had paid the captain to take it off their hands and return it to the island where it had been fashioned. I trailed the story to the warehouse. Little did I know I had found an artifact that could actually tell me its tale." Finally, he smiled at her. Korina couldn't help but smile in return.

Often through the month-long journey, he called her forth. He had a portable game of Twin Stones and taught her to play. She couldn't move the pieces, but that allowed her to focus fully on the strategy as she told him which ones to move. Aiden praised her for how quickly she caught on.

When they weren't playing, they talked. Korina told him all about the muses and the other skills they had taught her. Aiden spoke of life in the palace. They compared childhoods and philosophies. Korina memorized everything about him, eager to learn more. The time with him was never enough. When he dismissed her each night, she distracted her empty heart by filling the surrounding emptiness. After many pots and vases of shadow clay, she began to mold her first figure—a likeness of the prince.

"We've just returned home. This mirror will have a special place in my chambers." Aiden reached toward the mirror, but lowered his hand before he touched its surface. "I wish I could spend all day with you, as I have been. I haven't had such a worthy opponent in Twin Stones for years. And I'll miss being away from your face, your voice. But I have duties now that I've returned. And I can't sit idle now that I can do something for you. I'll start by inquiring at court."

Korina didn't want to see him go, either, but knew she would never be free from the mirror if she kept him here. "Don't worry; I won't be going anywhere."

He laughed, brightening the firmness of his expression. "I promise to check in as oft as I am able."

She held the image of his smile long after he dismissed her.

Aiden visited her the first two evenings, with nothing new to report. Korina waited for his third visit, but it didn't come at the usual time. She strained between worry and hope. When she finally broke down, about to seek him with the mirror, he came. The morning sun just lightened the view outside his window, highlighting his distraught face.

"I returned home just in time to see my mother die." Korina yearned to reach out and wipe away the tears that stained Aiden's cheeks. "The wasting sickness finally took her. Father is berating me. He said I should have been here for her these past two years." He ran his hands over his face and up through his matted hair. "I'm a disappointment to him. With my brother Shane now in line for the Vernissia throne, I am to rule Arania. My father had hoped I would marry before my mother died, so he could step down from the throne and let me take over. Everyone thought I would return from the Outer Isles with a bride, like my cousin Marcos did, but all I brought home was a mirror." Aiden's eyes pierced Korina's heart. "They don't understand how special this mirror is. But it remains true that I need a bride. Korina, will you marry me when I free you from this prison?"

She flushed, unsure how to respond. He couldn't possibly marry her, she was too young. But no, he had traveled for nearly two years before awakening her. Four years trapped in this mirror. She would be eighteen now. "What if you cannot free me?"

His blue eyes hardened. "You need to trust me. I already gave you my word. Now, will you give me yours?"

Korina bit her lip. Her, married to a prince. And not any prince... Aiden, the man who distracted her from the darkness and quickened her heart. But if, by some miracle, he found a way to free her, then anything was possible. "I will marry you."

A grin lit up his face, and the twinkle returned to his eyes. "I'll resume my visit to court in a few days, learn what I can about Lady Sophia." He blew her a kiss. "Until next time."

With increased enthusiasm, Korina used the mirror to follow Aiden as he visited court, and mimicked his frustration as each and every lady he spoke with denied knowledge of Lady Sophia ever having a daughter. They knew of her pregnancy, but heard the babe was stillborn. Korina thought back to her time in the manor, never in her mother's presence, and ushered to her room when company came. Anna had told her the events would be too boring for an active child such as herself. That may have been the truth, but wasn't the real reason. Her eyes remained on Aiden as she hoped for a confrontation with Sophia herself. But it was not to happen that day. Aiden returned to his chambers.

Korina expected him to visit her at once, convinced their engagement would be enough for him to visit before the usual time.

With each following task, her disappointment grew. He stood with the king and made judgments on cases presented to them, played Twin Stones with his visiting brother, and wrote missives. When he began to strip for a bath, she flushed and quickly let the vision go. But the image of his bare chest lingered in her mind.

Three more vases, a pitcher, and a full bust of the prince sat beside her. He still hadn't come. Surely it wouldn't hurt to check in on him again. An entire day must have passed, or no time at all, as she caught him stepping out of another bath. Skin burning, she squeaked and spun around until she felt the mirror return to black. No more spying, she told herself. Even if she does somehow marry him, it's not right to view such private moments. "He asked me to trust him. So, I'll trust he comes to me when he has something to share." Nodding to herself, she busied herself again with the mist.

Surrounded by pots, statues, vases, how long had she been in this darkness? She had to get out. Her sanity depended on it. When would he talk to her? To quell her itch to see Aiden, Korina began to pull apart her creations. Only a few remained when he finally came.

"Mirror, open yourself to me."

She locked her eyes onto his when the mirror cleared.

"Why didn't you visit me?"

He appeared shocked. "I attended my mother's funeral rites last night."

"Oh... but you've bathed twice since you last came. Has it only been one day?" It felt like so much longer.

Aiden smirked. "You saw me bathe?" Her burning face must have been answer enough for him. "I forget you do not know all the customs. Royalty is not buried as are the commoners. My first bath was to prepare for the rites and ceremonies, to look my best as I bid farewell to my mother. The second bath was after the funeral pyre to cleanse myself of her ashes. Also to custom, guards watched over my bed all night to protect the future king. They would only think of sorcery if they saw me visit you. I am sorry."

Korina sighed in relief. It hadn't been his own choices that kept him away from her. "And did you learn anything new today?"

He shook his head. "No one knows of your existence, let alone your disappearance. Lady Sophia herself hasn't visited court for some time now. Were any of the household witness to the spell? As of now, I only have your word that she is your mother. I do not doubt you, but need more proof before confronting her."

"We were alone. But the staff saw me before I disappeared again. Surely someone knows something."

"As nobility cannot help me, I will look elsewhere. Servants talk. I think I'll dine in the kitchen next morn."

She gave him the names she knew: Anna, Meric, Janisen, and the rest. If they were lucky, at least one would have family here in the capital.

It took three days of gossip with the servants to track down someone who knew the story. A stablehand's best friend was the cousin of the wife of the son of the cook at Redcap Manor, and had heard rumors of a disappearance in the manor but didn't know details. The day after speaking with the stablehand, Aiden reported meeting with the cook's son himself, who owned a farm a short carriage ride outside the capital.

"He remembers well the week you disappeared. It's the same week his daughter was born. His mother came to help while his wife rested, but couldn't stop speaking about you. Said their precious Snow had been thought dead for years, then suddenly returned with a magical tale of living with the muses. But that same night, her nurse went to check on her and she was nowhere to be found. The lady of the house said she ran away, but the girl's belongings were still in her room—all the beautiful gifts that proved her story of the muses true. The staff hid her things before they, too, could disappear."

"Did no one look for me?"

"They did. But your mother convinced some that you must have run away. The others eventually gave up. Most don't like Sophia, but the manor is their home, and she ignores them. She's never acted cruel, merely uncaring."

Korina leaned her head on the glass. "Did they wonder why you asked about me?"

Aiden traced the outline of her face with his fingertips. "Yes. I told them I had heard rumors and wanted to bring justice if they were true. That pleased them. And it is the truth." He grinned, causing Korina's heart to flutter. "I feel confident confronting her now. She holds elaborate parties at her manor regularly. I'm sure she'd be flattered if I attended one, but I don't want to meet on her terms. If she lived closer, I'd make a surprise visit. But it would draw too much notice now for me to spend a few days away from the capital. I'll summon her to the palace-"

"But she won't confess. She's too proud. And if you show her the mirror as proof, she'd simply laugh. You could summon her staff as well, but it would either make her suspicious or she'd simply bring those that trust her."

Aiden frowned, ran a hand through his hair. "We need a solid plan, as well as a fitting judgment."

"Ask the mirror."

"Oh. That sounds simple. Why didn't we think of that before?"

"You're a prince. You're not used to taking 'truth' at face value. That's why you wanted proof backing up my story."

He gazed at her, eyes lit from within. His words caressed her. "You see much truth without the aid of the mirror." He cleared his throat. "Mirror, how do we bring justice to Korina?"

Nothing. Korina sighed. "That's too close to the heart of its magic. Anytime I wished to see the spell that trapped me here or how to gain my freedom, the mirror closed itself. It will not answer that. Try asking for something different."

The prince drew his brows together for a moment. "Mirror, what do we need to confront Lady Sophia?"

The familiar pressure of words not her own filled Korina's throat, and she spoke. "Use she who was cast out."

Aiden's next words overflowed with hope. "Mirror, where do we find this woman?"

"The one who freed her promptly deserted her. She drifts alone." The image of the dark woman filled the air between them, and they saw her begging on the steps of a wide brick building.

Aiden laughed. "I know that place. That's the Mason Hall in the next town over. I had to go resolve a dispute there the year before I left. Father can attend court himself for now. My duties can wait; I'll seek this woman immediately. I may be gone a few days, but should not be alone when I return." Aiden pressed his fingers to the mirror in farewell.

Korina trembled with anticipation. The woman may have conspired to trap her, but they shared the experience of being alone in the mists. The thought crossed her mind that the woman may have been trapped for a reason, an evil contained, but it was just as likely that she had as innocent a soul as Korina. She hoped Aiden would hurry.

While she waited, she watched her mother in the mirror. So confident, and as beautiful and vain as ever. Four years had not changed her. Lady Sophia held one of her events the next day, a fox hunt in the woods. It reminded Korina of her single hunting trip, or, more appropriately, being the hunted, and she could not watch more.

Korina held her breath when the prince summoned her again, the woman appearing at his side. Three days since she had seen him, yet this time her eyes were drawn to the brown ones before her. Those eyes met hers, and held for a time in silence. The Outer Isles woman looked older. She still wore her black cloak, but dust coated the surface and the clothes beneath had torn and faded. The skin of her round face pulled tight at her eyes and mouth. Korina spoke first. "You told Sophia the spell, didn't you."

The woman nodded.

"Why?"

"I had been within the mirror for sixteen years. I have my own redemption to seek and I saw a way out. Would you not do the same?"

Sixteen years... Korina thought four an eternity. "Will you help me then...?"

"Fatinah. My name is Fatinah. The spell would require someone to take your place. Are you ready to curse someone with that?"

Aiden spoke for the first time since greeting the mirror. "I know someone that deserves such a fate. She should be acceptable, as she betrayed you both."

Korina understood. "My mother."

Fatinah cocked her head. "But Lady Sophia already knows the curse. Who is to say she won't trick someone into releasing her?"

"I assume the mirror can't be broken, or she would have done so after trapping Korina."

"You assume correctly."

Her mind raced until it collided with the memory of her first question she asked the mirror. "Reunite her with my father."

"Your father still lives?" Aiden asked.

Korina shook her head. "No, he died before I was born. His body lies in the sea."

Aiden smiled. "Ah, so we drop it into the ocean. Perfect. No one will find and free her there. Your quick ideas will come in handy as my queen."

She blushed. Marriage to the prince suddenly seemed a real possibility. They left her with those thoughts as each began their role. Aiden went to summon Lady Sophia for an audience with the prince, while Fatinah sought the components for the spell.

Korina scanned the private audience chamber outside the mirror. A padded throne sat just in view to her right. A blue cushioned settee lounged a comfortable distance ahead, facing both the throne and the mirror. She knew Fatinah knelt directly behind the mirror, prepared to cast the spell.

Aiden pressed his hand to the glass, and Korina did the same, wishing she could feel his skin. He must have seen her longing. "Soon, my love." His passionate gaze burned within her, and she held his words as he covered the mirror with a golden cloth without dismissing her. Korina bit her tongue as the knock came. She listened carefully to the muffled voices, eager not to miss anything.

"Enter."

The door creaked, then after a moment clicked shut.

"Your Highness," Lady Sophia said. "I am humbled to be in your presence. What do you require of me?"

"Please, sit. You must know I need a bride if I am to take the throne."

"But of course. Do you mean to ask me about one of my acquaintances? I've spent much time with the young ladies at court."

"Lady Sophia, you do not understand. Surely I would want the fairest queen by my side. No other lady at court can match your splendor."

"My L-l-liege, surely you don't mean to marry me? I am far from the youngest-"

"Do you disagree with me? Is there someone here that surpasses your beauty?"

"N-no, my Lord."

It pleased Korina to hear her stutter. She had never seen her mother's composure shaken. Though she still couldn't see it, at least Aiden allowed her to listen.

"Then, in honor of the engagement, I have a gift for you."

A moment passed, and Korina held her breath. The cloth fell away, and she met the startled gaze of Lady Sophia. "Hello, Mother."

Sophia cried out as Fatinah began the chant. "No! You wretched girl. You've been a curse to me since you grew in my belly and drove my husband away." She threw herself at the mirror, but her beating fists were pulled flat as Korina put her hands up. Glass dissolved, and she wrapped her fingers to dig her nails into the backs of Sophia's hands. The dark mist billowed up and out to surround them both. Sobs overcame Korina as the hands in hers disappeared with the mist. She heard a scream as her legs collapsed and Aiden's arms surrounded her. This time, the darkness that engulfed her was a sweet and comforting one.

Korina awoke on the settee with her prince standing above her.

"Are you well?"

"Hungry, and desperate for some real clothing, but free and well."

He leaned over and kissed her. His lips were warm and firm, and oh so wonderfully solid. She hungered for more than food. Now that she found love, she did not want to be apart from it. How could she have dismissed it as unimportant?

"Come, let us find you a gown and get you fed, so I may present you to my father as my future bride."

"Where is Fatinah?"

"She's with some of my men, preparing to leave on the next ship. I have instructed them to dispose of the mirror on their way to take her home. I gave her funds to help her restart her life."

Epilogue

Once Korina adjusted to a normal schedule of meals and sleep, Prince Aiden presented her to the king, who then presented her to the people. With no reason to wait, the marriage took place the following week, followed by a coronation. By the day of the wedding, Korina's tale had traveled all the way up to Lesenti. The muses, abashed that they let her out of their care to such a fate, but pleased with the karmic outcomes, attended the wedding with gifts anew, that the new queen would have all the trappings befitting her new station.

Korina's time with the muses, and her knowledge gained while watching people through the mirror, helped shape her into a woman fit to be queen. One of her first acts was to convert Redcap Manor into a home for abandoned children and those who left troubled homes. The staff had the option to work for the new establishment, retire with ample wages, or join Korina's entourage at the palace. Anna took the latter option, becoming the nursemaid for the princess born two years later.

Author's Note

Mirror is my Snow White tale. I have a thing for mirrors, being trapped behind glass. Maybe it's an introvert thing, feeling like internally I'm yelling and pounding to be seen, but not being heard. Anyway. This solved a few things for me, combining the glass coffin and the mirror, giving the person in the mirror her own backstory, and giving my Snow a way to still interact with the world. Like Sleeping Beauty, the traditional tales are all being woken with a kiss from a stranger. Ugh. Let the girl fall in love!

This story ties in closely with *The Blazing Princess*. Korina watches the story play out, and Aiden's story continues here. It gives a brief first mention of the Outer Isles and the Old Ones. It is also our first glimpse of the Sky Realm, particularly Lesenti, home of the muses.

My initial notes:

> snow white. what if I combined snow white and the other side of the mirror? a girl is trapped in the mirror. only way she can leave is if someone else takes her place. that's why she helps the queen, telling her how to find Snow White. rather than eating an apple, falling into a coma, and being placed in a glass coffin, she is captured and put in the mirror. then the mir-

ror is sold so the queen doesn't have to see her daughter. but a prince buys the mirror and together they arrange for the queen to take Snow White's place. then the mirror is destroyed so she is trapped forever. what happens to the other girl? does she live happily ever after? don't want to use seven dwarfs. who else could Snow White go to? what would be a good name for her? seven spirits? fairies? or do I want to connect it to my other tales, and use the seven muses? then the question would be if the tale fits into the world I've already created. with my image of being trapped in another world in Blazing Princess, and her beating on the solid lake, I think it would work.

The girl in the mirror, Fatinah: Arabic name for "Fascinating, captivating, alluring, enchanting". Why was she imprisoned? That gets answered in a later tale.

The Princess Test

Mary W. Jensen

Contents

1

After a fever defeated King Ramon's frail body, the kingdom of Senatin expected Prince Marcos to marry and take the throne. The eldest child, Rosa, had already abdicated by her refusal to marry. Instead of complying with expectation, Marcos disappeared. As tradition was only for a married couple to rule, Queen Adriana stepped aside and her daughter Selena stepped up as regent, with her nobleman husband, until Marcos was either pronounced dead, officially gave up his right to the throne, or married and took his rightful crown.

Marcos had sailed the seas and the Outer Isles for a year before coming to Teluk-malu, Zuleika's island home. He claimed to be a merchant. He told her of the loss of his father to illness, and how he didn't feel ready to walk in his footsteps. He made no mention of a crown.

Marcos and Zuleika fell in love, drawn together as the tides to the shore. He didn't tell her his whole truth until he proposed. Not a merchant, a prince! And he wanted her to be his queen. But if she were the ocean tides, he was her shore. Her home. And so she left hers for his.

Zuleika marveled at all the stone and people as their carriage entered the city. It seemed her entire island could sit within the city walls. They were so far inland that she could no longer hear or smell the ocean. She hadn't thought that was possible. She wished her Amah had ridden with them at least, but she would arrive later with their luggage. Marcos hadn't wanted to wait for them to unload the ship before rushing back home. And so far, everyone she had seen was of Marcos' dusky complexion, or paler. She didn't see anyone as dark as herself.

They pulled into the courtyard of the castle proper. She had never seen a castle before, only heard of them in stories. It loomed over her, blocking out the setting sun.

Marcos stepped out of the carriage, then turned to lift her down. His grip was solid, grounding her. He leaned down to kiss her gently. "You'll be fine. I'm right here."

He continued to hold her hand as they walked up the stone steps. An older man in red and black livery opened the grand doors and escorted them inside. "A pleasure to see you returned, master Marcos."

"Thank you, Darius."

"Court is just winding down in the assembly hall. Your mother already retired for the evening, but both your sisters are in attendance."

Their footsteps echoed in the stone corridor as they followed the man.

"I look forward to seeing them," Marcos said.

"And who is your guest that I am to announce?"

Marcos introduced Zuleika as they approached another set of doors. Carved into the center of each door was a gemstone surrounded by a crown. The woodwork was beautiful, like something her father would have done. She wished she could have studied it longer, but Darius was already opening the doors. Marcos held her back while the older man entered the large chamber.

This must be the assembly hall. These doors entered one of the long sides. She saw benches in two rows on the left and a raised dais on the right.

Darius cleared his throat, and the murmur of voices hushed. "Announcing the return of Prince Marcos, with his new bride..." the herald paused, "Zuleika of Teluk-malu."

She couldn't hear the whispers of the onlookers, but she could see them huddled, talking.

With their announcement out of the way, Marcos pulled Zuleika into the grand room. They stopped in front of the dais. Marcos bowed, and Zuleika followed suit.

"Welcome home, brother."

Zuleika looked up to see a woman near her same age standing up from her tall-backed chair. A beautiful red gown billowed around her, diamonds and lace inlaid in intricate patterns, making the woman look like a jewel herself.

Marcos gestured up to the woman. "Zuleika, this is my younger sister Selena, and her husband, Antonio." The woman in red nodded graciously. Antonio sat beside Selena in an identical chair, rubbing his goatee. Marcos then gestured to the far side of the dais, where two more chairs sat, less detailed but no less cushioned. One chair remained empty. The other held a woman with a simpler dress, in a darker red, almost to the point of purple. "And this is my older sister, Rosa." Both women shared Marcos' dusky skin and dark brown hair.

Zuleika bowed again. "It is my pleasure to meet you all."

"I'm just glad my wayward brother has returned," Selena said. "And with a bride, no less! We must begin planning the wedding immediately."

"But we are already married," Zuleika said.

Gasps arose from the crowd.

Selena frowned. "Who blessed this marriage? Who officiated it?"

"My family gave their blessing. Our village elder performed the ceremony."

"That simply will not do. Marcos is royalty. Things must be done properly." She took a deep breath and waved her hand. "I apologize. This is not the time or place. You are still in your traveling clothes. Rest up and we will discuss arrangements tomorrow. The Emerald Suite should be guest ready. Darius, our head steward, will show you the way and ensure you have everything you need."

Traveling clothes? Zuleika picked at the folds of her embroidered skirt. Next to her wedding dress, this was the best thing she owned.

"This court is now dismissed, as we have much catching up to do." Selena pulled Marcos away down one hall, followed by Antonio.

Rosa took a moment to touch Zuleika's shoulder in passing. "I look forward to getting to know you, sister." Then she too left, leaving Zuleika alone with Darius.

"This way, Lady Zuleika."

Zuleika was fully lost by the time they reached her chambers. At least a plaque labeling the Emerald Suite adorned the door, directly across from the Opal Suite. She imagined all the rooms were named after gemstones. Her suite comprised a sitting room, dressing room, a spacious bedroom featuring a four-poster bed, and her own private bathing room. Everything in various shades of green. She wasn't sure she could get used to this opulence.

"We will bring your luggage as soon as it arrives. In the meantime, we have dressing gowns in the wardrobe. I will send a maid to draw your bath. Is there anything you require?"

"Will Marcos be joining me?"

"The prince resides in his own chambers in the Royal Wing."

So she would be alone tonight. In a strange new place. "My Amah, she should arrive with my luggage. Will you send her to me?"

"Is she your servant?"

Zuleika laughed, picturing her Amah taking orders from anyone. "No, she is my mother's mother, and helped to raise me after my mother's death."

Darius nodded his apology. "I will have the Ruby Suite prepared for her at once."

She would never find her in this maze, and she could already see Amah scoffing at all the unnecessary space of her own suite. "The bed is certainly large enough; can she not stay here with me?"

"We have adjoining chambers just off the sitting room, normally for personal maids." He showed her the door hidden behind a tapestry that led to a much smaller room with a washbasin and sturdy bed.

"That should be fine. Thank you."

There was nothing for Zuleika to do as she awaited her bath. Her luggage was still being delivered, and there were no books or games visible. She collapsed upon the settee in the sitting room. At least she could be comfortable in her boredom. Her mind wandered to Marcos. What was he doing? She hadn't even been able to wish him good night. No one had forbidden her from seeing him; she just needed to find him. If only she had thought to ask Darius before he left. Any maid should be able to direct her. She merely had to find someone.

Fortunately, the door wasn't locked. She hadn't imagined they would lock her in her room, but she also hadn't expected to have her own chambers away from her husband. So, she wandered the halls. The royal wing was likely on the opposite side of the castle than the guest wing. So focused was she on the plaques, trying to remember her route to return, she stumbled right into someone.

The collision resulted in a clatter and an exclamation from whomever she had bumped. Zuleika stepped back and regained her balance.

The woman, likely a maid, dressed simply in a blue cotton dress with her hair tucked into a headscarf. She had been carrying a large clay jar filled with water, which was now in pieces. The maid knelt to clean the mess as the water quickly spread across the stone floor.

"How clumsy of me. I am so sorry. Let me help."

The maid cried out, having cut herself on one of the finer pieces.

Zuleika looked around but saw no linens. This was all her fault in any case, so it was fitting she sacrifice her own dress. She tore a piece off the hem, careful to avoid the nicer of the embroidery. She knelt down and took the maid's pale hand in her own. "Let me." She pulled a shard from the maid's palm, then wrapped the cloth around the wound.

The maid looked up, strands of red curls slipping from her scarf. "Are you not the new princess, Marcos' bride?"

"I am." She tied off a knot to secure the make-shift bandage.

"Surely this is beneath you. I am beneath you." She pulled her hand away. "Allow me to finish here. These were steeped herbs meant for your bath. I am sorry for messing it up. I will get a new jar."

"You will do no such thing. I would never ignore someone in need. And this is as much my fault, if not more." Zuleika tore another strip off her dress and used it to soak up the herbal water, then scooped up the remaining pieces of pottery. "Where can I dispose of these?"

"The kitchens. This way."

Zuleika followed the maid to the kitchens and put the pieces of the jar and the torn cloth in the indicated bin. "I was looking for my husband, for Prince Marcos, but it seems I should retire instead." Especially with her now torn dress. She turned back to the maid. "I'm sorry again for my clumsiness. I hope your hand will be fine."

"Do not apologize. You showed genuine compassion this night." The air shimmered, and the maid stood taller, no longer garbed in drab clothes, but in a brilliant green gown, her red hair a radiant halo.

Zuleika gaped in wonder. "Are you the moon goddess, Delwyn?"

"No. But I am one of her daughters. My name is Tesni; I am the muse of compassion. The Outer Isles are not part of our dominion, but we have been following Marcos' journey. You may not have been blessed at birth, but you have proven yourself worthy." Tesni clasped her hands, now unbandaged and whole, and opened them to reveal a large walnut. "Within this shell are three dresses. The first you will receive is blessed by my sister Meinir, muse of elegance. The second is blessed by Anwen, muse of beauty. The third is blessed by my sister Enid, muse of life and wisdom.

Zuleika took the walnut shell and held it delicately. "Three dresses? What would I need so many for?"

"You will know when the time comes." Tesni cupped Zuleika's hands in her own and closed them over the walnut shell. She leaned over and placed a warm kiss on Zuleika's forehead. "Remember your worth."

Zuleika closed her eyes to hold back tears from the wonder and awe of being in a deity's presence. They didn't have many tales of the muses back home, and she had certainly never expected to receive a gift from one.

When she opened her eyes, she was back in front of the doors to the Emerald Suite. Had she imagined everything? She still held the walnut shell and rubbed her fingers over its grooves. It felt real. Her dress had certainly been torn. Could this small shell really hold three dresses? She opened the door to her chambers to find her Amah within.

"Amah!" She rushed forward to throw her arms around her loved one. "Oh, how I've missed you."

"You saw me just this morning, girl. What is all this fuss about?"

Zuleika laughed. "It has been such a long day." She told her Amah everything that had happened since she arrived and showed her the walnut shell.

"Quite a day, indeed. And look at your dress! Your luggage is in your room, and your bath is prepared. Take this off and I'll see what I can do to re-hem it while you bathe."

Zuleika stripped down to her shift, leaving the damaged dress in her Amah's care. The cedar chest they had left at the foot of her bed. All her belongings in one box. She sifted through her things until she found her jewelry box, palm wood carved with hibiscus flowers, her mother's favorite. It had been a gift from her father to her mother on their wedding day. Mother had passed away when Zuleika was still a young child. On her own wedding day, Zuleika wore a crown of hibiscus flowers in her memory, and her father passed on the jewelry box so she would have something to remember both her parents. She wished Papa could be here now. She tucked the walnut shell in the box, then set it on the vanity table near her bed.

The next morning, Darius returned to escort Zuleika to breakfast. "And is my Amah invited as well?"

"But of course, ma'am." The dining hall, he explained, was the one for the royal family and private guests. They had a larger common room for bigger gatherings.

Colorful tapestries warmed the cold stone. A red table runner ran the length of a long oak table. The royal family had already taken their seats. A woman she hadn't met yet, with gray-streaked dark hair pulled into a long braid, sat at the head next to an empty chair. Marcos sat directly to her right. Selena and Antonio sat to her left, then Rosa. Then a teenage boy with a messy head of hair. Darius gestured Amah to sit across from Rosa and pulled out the chair next to Marcos for Zuleika. She was glad to see everyone more casually dressed, as she wore a simple yellow cotton dress herself. A breakfast buffet sprawled across the table.

Marcos leaned over and kissed her cheek. "Good morning, lovely. Did you sleep well?"

"Like sleeping on a cloud."

Marcos pointed at the boy. "This sulker is my brother, Nicolas. Give him a few more hours to fully wake up." Then he gestured to the woman at the head of the table. "This is my mother, Adriana."

Zuleika bowed her head in respect. "You have raised a wonderful son. It is my pleasure to finally meet you."

Adriana smiled warmly. "Welcome to our table. I look forward to getting to know you. Now help yourself to some breakfast while we talk about wedding plans."

After last night, Zuleika didn't bother bringing up the fact of her island wedding. Marcos didn't speak up, so this must be custom. She would simply enjoy marrying him all over again.

They set the wedding for one month's time. Royalty from the other three kingdoms would be invited. A royal wedding was much more complicated than an island one. But she had Marcos and Amah to help her through.

Marcos squeezed Zuleika's hand. "And after the wedding will be the coronation, and you will finally be my queen."

Antonio spoke up for the first time during the meal. "How do we know she is fit to rule? Not only is she a stranger, but she is also a commoner, and a foreign one at that."

Marcos burst up from his seat. "She has a name. Do you not trust me to choose a bride fit to rule by my side?"

Zuleika stiffened, unsure how to react.

Antonio scraped back his chair as he stood to meet Marcos's gaze across the table. "You abandoned your country for two years!

Selena and I have been ruling in your stead. Then you return with no warning, with this dark-skinned peasant, and expect everyone to welcome you with open arms. My wife is the one who has done the work. Given her time and her focus to this country. And now you want to take the crown from her!"

Zuleika felt like shrinking and disappearing into her chair. He was right; she was no princess. No ruler.

Adriana stood and slammed the table. "Enough! I do not like this squabble at my table. Selena, is that how you feel as well?"

Selena nodded coolly. "I feel I have been a fair ruler. Marcos made his choice two years ago. Why should we have to change everything now?"

"A series of tests, then," Adriana said, "to see if Zuleika is worthy. If she passes, she will be crowned, no more disputes. Do you all agree?"

Marcos nodded, then Selena, and finally Antonio. Adriana looked to Zuleika. "Do you agree to this?"

"What if I fail?"

"If you fail, or if you choose not to test yourself, then you will never hold the crown." Adriana looked to her son. "Then Marcos may decide if he wishes to relinquish the crown and remain married to you without the title. Or you return to your island alone."

"Then I have no choice. I will take your tests."

Adriana nodded. "Then the wedding plans will continue for now. And we shall plan your tests to coincide."

Three events would take place in the week prior to the wedding. They would seem to the guests as normal parts of the wedding planning. Yet each would contain a test for Zuleika, to prove she could be a graceful and noble ruler, and not embarrass the Senatin royal family. Zuleika would not know the specifics of each test, only the event they would take place within. On the first night, a royal ball. Followed by a feast the next evening. The third day, a session of court, where the people could speak directly to their potential new queen. Finally, on the fourth day, the wedding, and, if Queen Mother Adriana deemed Zuleika worthy, a coronation. Only a few weeks to learn how to be royalty.

After the announcement, Rosa found Zuleika sitting in the kitchen. "I have been looking for you. Are you well?"

Zuleika fiddled with a piece of broken pot. "I don't know. It's all so very much to take in. I feel more comfortable here than with your family. What if I really don't belong?"

Rosa put a hand on Zuleika's shoulder. "Royalty is truly a heavy burden. One I have managed to avoid."

"Why did you never marry and take the throne?"

Rosa pulled up a stool. "A mixture of reasons, I suppose. One must be married to rule in Senatin, and I simply do not see the appeal."

"Have you never been in love?"

"No. I have felt no physical or emotional draw to a man or a woman. I am happy simply being alone. And I would not wish to marry for duty alone, if I could not give my partner the affection they deserve. So early on I abandoned the idea of being queen, and I find other ways to help my people."

"What do you do?"

"I'm a teacher. I tutor our city's noble children, and I spend my Enisdays in the low village with any children who wish to join me in the square."

"Enisday?"

"Sixth day of the week, a day of reflection to honor the beloved Enid. A week is Tinsday through Crysday."

On the islands, they lived in the moment, each day as it came. Here, even the days were structured and named. She felt the potshard dig into her palm and she took a deep breath to force herself to relax.

Rosa reached out to take the shard from Zuleika, set it back in the bin, and took her hand. "You have much to learn. Allow me to help you. Do you dance?"

"I have danced on the beach, around a bonfire." She remembered her wedding night, twirling and moving with the light of the fire, the feel of the wind, bonding with Marcos.

"So nothing formal, like a galliard or a volta."

"Those are foreign terms to me."

"Do you have a ballgown?"

Zuleika remembered her last time in the kitchens, the gift she had received. The muse had said the walnut shell contained three dresses. Three dresses, one for each of her tests. "I think I may just have something that would work."

"That's settled then. During the days, you will plan your wedding, and at night I will meet you in the Opal Suite for practice. It is directly across from your own and tends to be reserved for the twins from Arania. As they won't be here for another two weeks, it will be empty."

So, during the days, Zuleika met with florists and dressmakers, usually accompanied by Adriana. Marcos insisted she got Crysday off, honoring the muse of love, to sweep her away on dates. He apologized for not spending more time with her, having his own wedding preparations and royal duties that he had neglected. He'd been making amends with his sister Selena as they reviewed the state of the kingdom. But this one day a week was for Marcos and Zuleika alone; they would walk in the gardens, or stargaze, or splash in the courtyard fountain. These reminders of his playfulness and care for her anchored her through the storm of activity for the rest of the week.

Her evenings she spent in the Opal Suite, where Rosa had the furniture pushed to the sides of the room for more room to dance. Once her feet tired, they would go over everything from etiquettes of nobility, to things such as days of the week which even a child here would know. Then, in the late hours, Rosa would call for wine and tell stories about her time out in the city, the people she would interact with. Zuleika returned to her room, exhausted. Her Amah would brush her hair, rub her sore feet, and wish her good night. And each night before bed, Zuleika held the walnut shell and repeated Tesni's missive: "Remember your worth."

By the week of the wedding, all the royalty of the other kingdoms of Tessagonia had arrived for the festivities. King Augustus and Queen Lorelei of Vernissia came with their young daughter. From Arania, King Shamus and Queen Naomi, with their twin sons. King Ivan and Queen Klera of Kether attended with all five of their children, ranging from the twenty-two-year-old Stephen to the little Natalia. The morning of the ball was an informal rehearsal, where Zuleika met the other royalty, and would at last get to practice her steps with Marcos instead of Rosa.

Overwhelmed by all the introductions, Zuleika found a nook with a small chair to take a breather while she waited for the dance instructor. She could hear some of the young princesses gossiping, just out of sight.

"Marka heard from Nicolas, Marcos' younger brother, that Adriana didn't plan this ball as a celebration." The voice lowered until it was just audible to Zuleika. "It's a test to see if his bride is worthy of being Queen."

Another girl piped in. "She *is* from the Outer Isles. They are so dark and primitive. If she makes a fool of herself, then Marcos won't be crowned, and Selena's rule will be permanent."

Zuleika clenched her fists, nails digging into her palms. It was bad enough with Queen-Mother Adriana judging. Now she knew everyone's eyes would be on her. The male partners arrived, and Zuleika waited until she heard the giggling girls move away before coming out of the shadow.

Marcos found her and pulled her into line. She had the steps down, but felt stiff and awkward. Marcos chided her to stop looking at her feet. Her thoughts were consumed by how others would react if she messed up. She was happy when the rehearsal was over and she could retreat to her chambers.

Dinner was a light meal served in her room. One mustn't dance on a full stomach. Her stomach was fluttering with too many nerves to eat much of the salad, anyway. She ran her fingers over the carved flower of the jewelry box. "I wish you were here, mother."

Her Amah, standing behind her, gently squeezed her shoulders. "She is surely watching over you now. As are the muses who have imparted their gifts. Now don't leave me waiting. I've been itching to see these supposed magical dresses."

The first you will receive is blessed by my sister Meinir, muse of elegance.

Zuleika lifted the lid of the jewelry box and retrieved the walnut shell. She pulled apart the two halves. A dress exploded onto her lap. The fabric was midnight blue, with diamond beadwork covering the bodice, and more scattered across the flared skirt like stars in the night sky. Blue ribbon lined the hem and decorated the matching slippers she found hidden in the dress's folds. "Thank you, muses, for thinking of everything." Amah helped her into the dress. It fit perfectly, hugging from neck to waist, flaring out to float as she gave a spin. Her arms were bare. She felt so regal.

A servant came to escort Zuleika to the ballroom. She recognized the gesture this time, to pause and await her announcement. After her introduction, she entered a grand hall filled with people looking her way. The other royals were already in attendance, as well as many unfamiliar faces. As the guest of honor, she had been the last to arrive. Thankfully, Marcos came to her, so she didn't have to find him in the crowd.

"You look stunning."

She smiled, reminding herself to relax. She had Marcos' confidence in her, as well as that of the muses. The first dance would be just the two of them, showing off their chemistry and connection. As they glided across the dance floor, she could feel Meinir guiding her steps. Marcos held her gaze, as if they were the only ones in the room. Through twirls and lifts and chassés, he courted her again. So happy, a laugh bubbled up as the music ended. Marcos kissed her to applause.

The second dance was that of the royals, a faster paced dance with fancy footwork and trading of partners through the song. At one point, Zuleika found herself dancing with Antonio. His footwork was uneven, and she nearly tripped as he pushed her too quickly into a turn, but she felt the dress steady her, keeping her in form and in step. His eyes narrowed as they switched partners again. Thanks to Meinir's grace, she got through the rest of the dance. Hopefully, it was enough. Marcos assured her she was the star of the dance floor.

The following night, Zuleika prepared for the celebration feast. *The second is blessed by Anwen, muse of beauty.* She wasn't sure how Anwen would help, or what the test could be. Yet there were three nights of events and three dresses. That surely wasn't a coincidence. The second dress spilled into her lap. It flowed like golden honey, soft and warm as the sun on her face on a summer's day. A delicate ribbon of coral pink lined the inner wrists of the long sleeves.

The feast took place in a much larger hall than the one she had been sharing her meals with the royal family. One long table sat on a dais overlooking a sea of smaller tables. Buffets lined the sides of the room, but Marcos assured Zuleika that those at the royal table would have servers. Amah hugged her before finding a seat with the people below.

Only one side of the long table had seating, so everyone could look up and see Zuleika eating. She was hoping to sit by Rosa, but Antonio filled the seat instead. Hopefully she wouldn't have to make conversation. At least she had Marcos on her left. She turned her chair slightly to angle toward her husband. He lifted her hand and kissed it. "You look absolutely radiant. The gold of your dress compliments your beautiful dark skin."

A fleet of servers in red and black livery set out the first course—a green pea pottage—for the royal table. Zuleika followed Marcos' cue on which spoon to use. The high neck of the dress reminded her to keep her head high rather than slouch over her dish, retaining her posture. The soup was delicious and helped her forget her fluttering nerves.

The second course was a platter of beef, pork, venison, salmon, and a second batch of servers to fill the goblets with red wine. She rehearsed the rules Rosa had taught her. No talking with food in your mouth, wash your fingers between courses, and don't touch the food directly on the platters, use a knife. The beef looked tender, so she used her knife to stab it and put it on her plate before tearing a piece off to eat. She would have to thank the kitchen staff for such an excellent meal. As she reached for her goblet, Antonio reached for a second serving of salmon. He bumped her elbow and wine sloshed out, spilling onto her dress. Before she could react, the liquid slid right off the slick fabric, leaving nary a stain. Thank you, Anwen. Antonio grumbled an apology.

The main course was a bird she was unfamiliar with. It had a long neck and served whole, for each person to cut off their own portion that they preferred. Zuleika cut off a leg, as she preferred the dark meat. It tasted similar to the wild turkeys they had on her island.

Thankfully, dessert came next, rather than another round of food, as she wasn't sure how much more she could eat. The bakers had outdone themselves, creating masterful displays of pastries that looked like colorful birds. They were filled with a sweet berry jam. Zuleika took extra care to take delicate bites and not spill the jam. Her dress may have repelled liquid, but it may not handle sticky jelly.

The evening ended with a performance by a team of acrobats. The first row of tables was cleared and pushed aside for the performers to do their flips and launch each other into the air. It gave her stomach a moment to settle before she had to return to her room. Marcos held her hand during the performance. She hoped she had done him proud again.

The third is blessed by my sister Enid, muse of life and wisdom.

The last dress to pool out of the walnut shell was a soft gray as the moon, with a silver ribbon highlighting the empire waist. Today Zuleika would be presented before the court. While usually reserved for nobles and wealthy merchants, this gathering welcomed any citizen with a petition. Darius escorted Zuleika to the same assembly hall where she had first been introduced. Rosa sat in her same chair, the seat beside her filled by Queen-Mother Adriana. The two more detailed chairs that had held Selena and Antonio were empty, and the couple were sitting in some additional chairs on the right of the dais. The announcer waited until Marcos came down the hall to join them.

He took her hand and kissed her cheek. "Beautiful, as always."

"Prince Marcos and his bride Zuleika of Teluk-malu."

Marcos led her up the dais steps to the thrones and sat to her right.

The announcer stepped to the center of the room. "This is a special session of court. It is your opportunity to speak with your future queen. Let us proceed."

The first few groups to approach came merely to introduce themselves formally to her, listing their ranks or services. From the eyes of the crowd, many had come merely to gawk at this dark-skinned pretender to the throne, not to address any proper business. Some came with questions or disputes. Zuleika would listen to Marcos and calm her mind to be open to Enid's wisdom before responding.

A weary woman came forward, holding the hand of a young child of age six. As the woman was about to speak, the child broke free and ran up the dais steps. Darius stepped forward to intercede, but Zuleika waved him back.

The little girl stopped in front of Zuleika and rocked on the heels of her feet. Her dark eyes were wide and curious. "Hi! Are you a princess?"

Zuleika slipped out of her chair to kneel in front of the girl. "I'm married to a prince, so I suppose I am. What's your name?"

"Isabelle."

"What a pretty name for a pretty girl."

Isabelle smiled and reached out her hand, then stopped. "Can I touch you?"

"Yes." She put out her hand for the girl to touch.

Isabelle rubbed the back of Zuleika's hand. "Your skin is so dark! But it doesn't feel cold like the shade. It feels just like my skin!"

Zuleika smiled. "We're not so different."

The girl's eyes opened even wider. "Does that mean I can be a princess, too?"

Zuleika remembered the muse's words. Remember your worth. "It does. You don't have to have a crown to be a princess. You just have to act like one. Do you know how to do that?"

"Be pretty and nice, like you?"

"That's certainly a good place to start. Be graceful, and gracious—that means be thankful—and listen to those around you so you can learn and grow. And have a good heart. Do you think you can do that?"

"Yes!"

"Then you will be a great princess. Now go back to your mother."

Isabelle ambushed her with a quick, yet fierce, hug, then rushed back down the steps.

Her mother blushed furiously as she took hold of the girl's hand again. "I am so sorry. I don't know what to do with her most of the day."

"Don't apologize." Zuleika stood up and brushed off her dress before sitting back down. "Now, what was your concern?"

"I need resources. Support. My husband died in an accident at the diamond mine, and we were compensated, but I still struggle. I am a seamstress and my little one is constantly underfoot. I would work when my husband was home and could help with Isabelle. But now it's all on me."

"What do children normally do during the day?"

"As they get older, they help more around the house, learn a trade."

Zuleika thought of Rosa teaching the children, and of her own sessions back home with a teacher each morning. She had an idea but hesitated whether it was her place to suggest such a grand feat. She glanced to Marcos, who nodded and smiled at her. This was her decision. She could feel Enid's reassurance, and Tesni's words to remember her worth. If she was to be queen, she must act the part. Not ask permission.

"What of a school? Do you have any common place the children can get education?"

"No. We could never afford a tutor. And most trades do not need a knowledge of reading or writing."

Her idea wouldn't be cheap, but it wasn't as if the royals didn't have funds to spare, with how fancy the rooms and the feasts were. She squared her shoulders and made her decision. "We should build a school. Free for the citizens of this city. In the morning, send the children to school. They can learn not just reading and writing, but arts and dance, that all may feel comfortable attending a royal ball, or improve their circumstances. In the afternoon, they can go to their apprenticeships and do their other work. With Gwynsday off, so youth still have the joy of play. Start them young, like Isabelle." She smiled at the girl. "Would you like to go to school and learn how to be a princess?"

Isabelle nodded vigorously. "Can I, Mama?"

"It sounds like a dream. I could work in the mornings, and my daughter could get an education." The mother looked at the others on the dais. "Is this possible?"

Marcos reached over to take Zuleika's hand. "I think it's a magnificent idea. Does that address your problem?"

"Yes, yes, thank you." The woman curtsied and hurried her daughter back to their seats.

3

Once the court concluded, Adriana stood and addressed her family.

"Now that the final task is done, I would like to see you all in my private audience chamber." She swept out of the room.

Marcos grumbled, "It was never a good thing getting called to Mother's audience."

"Should I be worried?" Zuleika asked.

"Of course not. Everything will be fine." But his furrowed brow betrayed him.

Zuleika bit her lip and held his hand tight as they followed the others.

The Queen-Mother's audience chamber was warmer than the assembly hall, both in actual heating with its fireplace, but also in decor. Instead of benches, plush divans and armchairs were strategically placed for conversation. There was also a tea table for more intimate conversations. A heavy desk took up one corner of the room. Adriana sat in a high-backed chair near the fireplace. "Sit please, everyone. Except for Zuleika. Come here, lass."

Zuleika moved to stand before Adriana, encircled by the royal family. Marcos stood by her rather than sit, which gave some comfort.

Adriana clasped her hands. "Zuleika, I have been watching you these past few days. Not always personally, but I am well informed. It is time to answer the question of your worthiness to the throne."

Marcos held up a hand to stall her. "Wait. Before you give your verdict, I have something to say." He turned to Zuleika and took her hands in his own. "I am sorry I haven't been able to spend more time with you these past few weeks. Crysday has been the highlight of my week. Seeing you these last few nights has given me much joy. When I asked you to marry me, you said yes to a man, not a prince. No matter what happens here, I will stay with you. You are my sun, my moon, my stars. You are my wife, and I love you."

His kiss calmed her racing heart. At least she wouldn't lose him.

Adriana cleared her throat, and the couple broke apart. "As I was saying. Zuleika, you have shown grace, composure, and wisdom. You bring a fresh voice to this land, and I believe you will do great things here. You have my blessing for the crown."

Zuleika's knees weakened. "Thank you. That is more than anyone could ask for."

Marcos tugged her back to face him. "But is it what you want? If you want to go home, I will give up everything here and go with you. Wherever we are, you will always be my queen. But will you be Senatin's queen?"

She thought of Rosa, who had helped her so much, of Isabelle and the other children. Perhaps she really could make a difference here. Make a home. "Yes, Marcos. I will rule by your side."

"Then I have one last order of business," he said as he turned to his younger sister. "Selena, you have ruled this country these past two years. I could use your knowledge if you will lend it. Will you be my adviser?"

Selena nodded regally. "It has been a relief to share my duties with you this last month. I hadn't realized the strain and bitterness I had been carrying. I gladly accept. And, perhaps stepping aside will allow me more time for my own family." She beamed as she placed a hand on her abdomen and reached out her other to clutch her husband's. A brief look of surprise came over Antonio's face, wiping away his typical glower.

Adriana smiled. "Then everything is settled. And many congratulations are in order. I suggest you all go get some sleep. Tomorrow is a big day."

The royal wedding was a full day of celebration. There was a parade, music, dancing, and sweets for all. The ceremony itself took place on a grand balcony overlooking the city, where all could witness, both nobility and commoner alike. The balcony had been turned into a garden paradise, lush with plants and flowers and lanterns. Marcos promised himself and his country to Zuleika, and for the second time she accepted him as her husband, their fates entwined as one. And they were crowned to the cheers of their people.

Zuleika took her first charge as queen to oversee the building of the new school. Naturally, she hired Rosa as the headmistress. Many of the children already knew her, and she was used to teaching. Zuleika had her Amah teach the children about the sea and the Outer Isles. She hoped it would make them more accepting of people who differ from themselves.

Author's Note

The Princess Test was originally going to be more of a Cinderella tale. But instead of focusing on the romance with the prince, I focused on the aftermath—how the family would react to a prince choosing a commoner. Here, it's also a bias against race.

This is my first tale that isn't a direct retelling of a single fairytale. It does, however, take elements from multiple tales. The base idea is a mashup of Cinderella (commoner marrying a prince) and Princess and the Pea (having to prove you're a real princess). The green pea pottage was also a nod to the latter story.

The three dresses come from Allerleirauh (also known as All-Kinds-of-Fur)—one as golden as the sun, one as silver as the moon, and one as shining as the stars. The dresses are all put into a nutshell in both that tale and The Iron Stove. Bride tests are also a common fairytale trope.

I try to keep it vague whether or not Antonio was sabotaging the tests. He's the one most against Zuleika becoming Queen. I didn't want him to become *too* much of a villain, so I gave him something else to focus on at the end of the story.

This is the first time we have reference to days of the week! I thought introducing the system to an outsider would be a great way to introduce it to a reader. And seven muses, seven days of the week, it was a natural fit. I did get some help from Facebook for adapting the muse names to a nameday. Here is the full list, as I don't believe they all show up in the tale:

Tinsday (Tesni)
Awnday (Anwen) – day of rest (beauty sleep)
Kaladay (Kala)
Menerday (Meinir)
Gwynsday (Gwynaeth) – no school, play day
Enisday (Enid) – teaching (day of reflection)
Crysday (Carys) – the day Marcos and Zuleika reserved for their romantic outings

Venom and Shadow

Mary W. Jensen

Contents

1

The Outer Isles circle the continent of Tessagonia. Within the southernmost cluster of islands is a volcanic island named Kalana, where starts our tale. The watchful eyes of the Sky Gods and their muse daughters rarely extend out so far. The islanders have darker gods, the Great Ones, to fear in their stead.

Hasahn left the bustle of the seaside behind, trekking inland. Most of the island providers were fishermen, but he preferred solid ground beneath his feet. The air was hot and humid under the late afternoon sun. Hasahn sighed, wishing it was already the cooler evening when the wild pigs are most active. He found a nicely branched tree overlooking an animal trail, perfect to set up his watch. He climbed onto a wide branch and leaned against the smooth tree trunk. Bow balanced across his lap, he opened his satchel to pull out a parchment-wrapped bundle. As he watched the underbrush, he ate the flatbread, jerky, and cheese his wife Fatinah had packed for him.

As the evening cooled, Hasahn finally heard the grunts of a wild pig. The long grass rustled, but the pig wasn't moving into view. Hasahn quietly notched an arrow. He called out a series of loud, guttural grunts. A large, hairy black boar waddled out of the grass toward him. Hasahn took aim and let loose his arrow. His aim was true, and the boar stumbled to the ground at the foot of the tree. The large boar would provide many meals. He would trade some of the meat for eggs and fruit and prepare more jerky for the days ahead.

Hasahn dropped his bow and slid down the tree, thinking of the upcoming feast. He did not see what else had awoken in the grass below him. As he reached down to grab his bow, a snake lifted its head and struck out, biting him on his wrist, then retreating to a coiled position. Hasahn left the bow beside the snake and stumbled toward the pig. The snake didn't follow, merely hissed in place. If he had brought his machete, they would have snake with their boar tonight. But he would leave it be and focus on his bigger prize.

Now that it was calm, he could see the snake was bright yellow, with orange stripes. It wasn't one he'd seen here before. Perhaps it had swum over from a neighboring island. The bite marks were red, but not deep. He took a cloth from his pack and wrapped it around his wrist. He'd clean the wound later; for now, he had a boar to deal with. He didn't fancy leaving his bow behind, but didn't want to risk getting bit again. The bow could wait; the boar wouldn't. The meat would start rotting in a few hours.

His wrist throbbed, but he managed to rope together the boar's feet and lift it over his head. One foot at a time, back down the mountain toward the village. Focusing on his steps helped distract him from the itch under the bandage. He flexed his left arm, feeling the tightness around the bite. The trees seemed to swarm around him, and he stumbled. The boar felt heavier, pulling him to the ground. Hasahn collapsed, unconscious. When he came to, the full moon already shone through the branches above him.

Fatinah would be worried. He had to get home. His arm felt stiff, but less painful than before. He ignored the discomfort and tried to stand. His balance was off and everything felt wrong. It took a moment for him to realize the boar was still slung around his shoulders. He wiggled out from under it and stood. The boar was too heavy to lift overhead again. He should have saved some food; his body must be weak from hunger. He tied a second rope to the one tied around the boar's feet. It would take longer dragging the boar behind him, but he refused to leave it behind.

He must have wandered off the trail before passing out. Nothing seemed familiar. Unsure which direction the path lay, he went downhill and listened for the sound of the sea.

Eventually, he came out on a cliff above the village. He hollered at some men below who were gossiping at the well. Once he drew attention to the boar, he quickly had three men climbing up to help him and the boar down to level ground. Two of the men hoisted the boar between them and headed for the hut Hasahn shared with his wife. The third asked Hasahn if he was well, but Hasahn waved him off.

His wife's joy at the sight of the boar doubled with the sight of her husband returned home. "I had worried, dear husband. But look at this feast you return with!"

Hasahn's arm throbbed as Fatinah embraced him, but he did not want to ruin the moment. She asked about the bandage, but he assured her it was just a scratch. Let her worry be done. If needed, he could seek the healer in the morning. Fatinah had prepared a hearty gruel, which he scarfed down. He would need his strength to carve the boar. Fatinah left to bargain out boar portions while Hasahn got to work. His left arm still smarted, but his right was fine and well. He asked the neighbor boy Pali to help with the work, as he was mostly working with one arm, sending the boy home with some of the meat as thanks.

It had been a long day, and the work had worn more on him than it should. Unable to focus, he collapsed into bed without even kissing his wife good night.

Fatinah woke to the familiar sounds of the village: merchants putting out their wares, fishermen heading out to sea. She cooked up some bacon to go with the usual gruel. Usually the aroma would wake Hasahn, but her husband slept on. Fatinah shook his shoulder, and he groaned but did not rouse. The man may have earned a day off from hunting, but surely he could still attend to his wife. Fatinah threw off the hides covering him and gasped. Hasahn's left arm had dark, webbed lines creeping up from his rough bandage. She pulled off the cloth to reveal two inflamed marks.

She shook Hasahn again until he finally opened his eyes. She let out a breath she didn't realize she was holding.

"Is it time to break fast?"

"We are going to the healer, you nut-head." Breakfast would have to wait.

Hasahn got out of bed, then stumbled a bit. Fatinah reached out to keep him from falling back down. "Just a bit light-headed."

"You fool, why didn't you say something sooner?"

He hung his head but allowed Fatinah to support him and guide him out. "I didn't want to worry you."

"And now your wound is worse off for it. Why are men so stubborn?"

The healer's hut sat in the middle of the village, next to the well. Fatinah pushed aside the palm fronds filling the doorway. Elder Koru sat cross-legged in the center of the circular hut, finishing his morning meditations. He opened his eyes as Fatinah lowered Hasahn to a pile of pillows.

The elder pulled his long black locks into a bun atop his head. "What brings you to my home today, Fatinah?"

"Hasahn has an infected wound. It looks as if tendrils of darkness are trying to consume him."

Elder Koru pulled a cord which opened a hatch overhead to let in more of the morning light. He gestured for Hasahn to show him the injury, hissing at the view. "This bite. Did you see what did it?"

"A snake," Hasahn replied.

"And what did this snake look like?" Elder Koru gently turned Hasahn's arm in the light. The dark veins traveled nearly up to the elbow.

"Bright yellow, with orange stripes."

"A sun viper. It has a deadly bite." He sighed.

Fatinah squeezed her husband's good hand. "Deadly? Is there nothing you can do?"

"This is not the first case I have seen. But I have only been able to save a man once. No medicine I have knowledge of will cure him. Only cutting off the injured limb before the venom burns up to his heart."

Hasahn paled. "Lose my arm? But what of my livelihood? How will I hunt with one arm?"

"It is the only way. I am sorry."

Fatinah held back her own tears. "And what happens if we don't? How long do we have?"

"You got bit yesterday, correct?"

"Yes."

"At most six days, then. If you are lucky."

"Then we do what we must." Fatinah turned her husband's face to hers. "I will work. And you could help with other tasks in the village. I would rather lose your arm than my husband."

Her husband slumped in defeat and rested his forehead against hers. "Anything to stay with my love."

Elder Koru gave his patient a mix of herbs to numb the pain. The couple waited, holding each other, suppressing their tears, as Elder Koru prepared and brought a young man to assist him. He sent Fatinah home to get Hasahn's own cleaver, the same he had used on the boar.

They tied Hasahn's upper arm with twine, then used the cleaver to chop off the infected arm at the elbow, where there was more tendon than bone. Hasahn bit down on a stick to allay his screams. Elder Koru used tongs to heat a stone. When he pressed it to the stump to seal the wound, Hasahn's strength gave way, and he passed out.

Fatinah woke early, after a restless night worried over Hasahn. She pulled the curtains back from the window to let in the morning light, then made a fire to heat water for tea and breakfast. Elder Koru had given them a tincture to help with the pain and healing, and a paste to apply each morning. The tincture smelled like bitter grasses when she opened it. She added it to the boiling water, then poured it into a clay mug to cool while she checked on Hasahn's wound.

The blanket over him was damp with sweat. Her husband shifted but did not wake as she attended to him. Elder Koru had wrapped a woven cloth around the stump. Last night, she wouldn't let Hasahn see her cry. His livelihood, his life, would not be the same. She cradled his poor arm, stifling her tears again, resolving to be strong. Elder Koru had warned her the arm may be red and swollen, but should be clean from infection if they had caught it in time. Fatinah bit her lip to avoid waking Hasahn as she unwrapped the wound. The stump was raw and red, and worst of all, black veins were already spreading again. Her tears fell free as she cradled his poor arm.

Elder Koru had said amputation was the only way to save him. If that hadn't worked, was he lost to her? Was it merely a matter of days before he was gone for good? She tenderly applied the paste, which smelled sweet like honey, and re-wrapped the stump. It may be pointless, but what else could she do? She hurried back to the healer.

Elder Koru was already up and eating porridge on a cushion outside his hut, facing the morning sun. He looked up at her distraught face and sighed, setting aside his porridge. "I take it he is not improving."

Fatinah shook her head and knelt before Elder Koru, the weight of the expected loss lowering her head nearly to his lap. She choked back a sob. "The black veins are back. Is there nothing else we can do? Could we... could we cut off more of the arm?"

He placed his hand on her head and stroked back her coarse hair. "I'm sorry, my daughter. I would not want to risk it. It is now beyond my knowledge."

"I would do anything! I cannot lose my husband." She sat up and pleaded. "Anything."

He hesitated a moment before responding. "As I said, there is nothing I can do. But perhaps..."

She sat a little straighter at the possibility of even a 'perhaps'. "Go on. Please."

"Have you heard of Aloka-pasar?"

Fatinah shook her head. "Is that a person? A place?"

"A grand market island. They have people coming in from all the Outer Isles, and from the mainland as well. If there are any new treatments, any advanced techniques, someone there would know."

"How do I find this... island market?"

"Aloka-pasar. All the traders know of it and travel through at some point. It is a hub for trade and travel. Go to the docks and ask for passage. It is a risk, though. The sun viper's bite is a seven-day death sentence. If what he told us is correct, you only have four days after this. He may be too weak to travel with you. Which would mean traveling to the market and back. Do you go on this shadow chase, in the slim hope you can save him? Or do you stay and spend your last days together at home?"

Fatinah's heart climbed into her throat. It wasn't much time. But Hasahn was her love, her life, her fire. She could not imagine living without him. "I must try. I will check the docks." She took his hands in hers and kissed them. "Thank you for all you have done for us. And for the hope you have given me."

2

F atinah stopped at the docks before returning home. The smell of the sea and the sound of the waves wrapped her in a familiar embrace as she waited before the lone boat. A crew of half-clad men were tidying the deck and moving cargo on and off the ship.

"Excuse me." She waved at one of the crew as they passed her by. He shifted the barrel he was carrying and glared at her.

"You're in the path, miss."

"I know. I just need to ask about passage."

"Not my problem, miss." He shifted the barrel again impatiently. "Have to speak to the captain."

She shifted to block him as he tried to move past. "And who is that?"

The sailor sighed and lowered his barrel. "Man with the cloak and spyglass. He's up top this time of day."

Fatinah looked toward the upper deck, where a young man was tidying ropes.

"No, up up."

She looked up further, gaze following a rope ladder up to a platform halfway up the central mast. An older man looked out at sea, his red cloak whipping in the higher air. "Oh."

She turned to thank the sailor, but he had already moved on. He had said nothing about staying off the ship, so she steadied herself and walked up the planked bridge, sidestepping more sailors. She stopped below the mast and looked up, shading her eyes. Too close to see the captain. How long until he came down?

"Hello? Captain?" No response. She should have asked for his name. Sailors moved around her, ignoring her. She eyed the rope ladder. Well, she did claim she'd do anything for Hasahn. No sense wasting time. She tied her skirt up and started climbing the ladder. It was less steady than she expected, and the wind grew stronger as she climbed. Halfway up, she called out again, unsure the captain could even hear her over the wind.

Just below the platform, she couldn't see how to best climb off the ladder and over the rail. She hollered again. "Captain?"

A head came over the rail, and he looked down at her. "You're not one of my crew. What in the deep are you doing here?"

"I need passage."

"Well, this is not the place to discuss such things. You would have been better waiting in my cabin."

If only someone had told Fatinah that, she would gladly have complied.

He shooed at her. "Git down then." He closed his spyglass and tucked it into a loop on his belt. "I'll be right behind you."

She looked down and gulped. It looked farther from this direction. Her feet searched for the next rung down, and she slowly wobbled her way toward the deck. Her hands hurt from gripping the rope. Down was harder than up, when she couldn't see where to put her feet and had to reach blindly.

The captain's gruff voice came from above. "By the deep, you are taking too long. I will see you down there." He swung past her, sliding down the mast like a tree trunk.

Fatinah tried to hurry her pace, but the faster she went, the more the rope swung. So she resigned herself to inching back down.

Her legs wobbled by the time her feet touched the deck. The boat wasn't even at sea, and she was already wishing for land. She better appreciated Hasahn's determination to not be a fisherman. The captain waved from an open door on the upper deck. Fatinah firmed herself and went to join him. The captain's cabin was well lit, with many windows and a covered ceiling lantern. The furniture was bolted to the floor. She glimpsed a bed behind some gauzy curtains. The captain gestured her to join him across a wide wooden desk. Large seashells acted as paperweights to hold down maps and charts.

The captain was an Outer Islander like herself, his dark skin weathered from his years at sea. His black hair was streaked with gray. He held out his hand for her to shake. "Captain Tanroa. Now where were you hoping to go, miss?"

"The market island. Aloka-pasar."

"A young lady like you heading to the shadow market alone? Are you sure?"

She bristled. "I am a grown woman and can take care of myself."

The captain shrugged. "You are in luck. We are heading that direction."

Her shoulders relaxed. "Good. How long will the trip be? When can we leave?"

"It's not far. We can be there within a day. Assuming we leave tomorrow, first thing in the morning."

A whole day lost. "Is there any way we can leave sooner? We have the whole day ahead of us."

Tanroa shook his head. "Did you not feel that wind? And see the sky? A storm is coming. We don't want to be caught in it. Best to wait it out."

It was not the news she wanted to hear. But she would not be the one sailing the ship. And there were no other ships. "I need to get there and back within four days. Is that something you can do?"

"This is a one-way trip. We head up–island and will be circling the mainland northward. You'll have to find a different ship that charters down–island for your voyage home."

She had no idea how long that would take. And if they left tomorrow, that only gave a day to get there, one to find a cure, and a day to return. Assuming she even found a ship traveling the right direction. And no way to test the cure until the last minute. Hasahn was weak, but she would have to risk his health declining and take him with her.

"Passage for two then. My husband will travel with me. What do you require for passage?"

"What do you have to offer? Can the two of you work?"

"My husband is... injured. But I can cook. I also have pork." The pork would do her no good rotting away in her hut, smoked or not.

"Meat other than fish is scarce at sea. Could you host us tonight?"

"Us?"

"The crew, of course. There be a dozen of us in total."

There was no way she could fit them all in her hut. The captain's bulk alone would make it crowded. "I don't have the space."

"Then could you come here? Feast with us on the ship this evening? Then you could sleep in a cabin here, and we would be on our way come morning."

"Yes, that will do. I have some preparations to make, but will be here tonight for supper."

"I'll have someone show you to the cabin and the kitchen. Then you can come on ship when you please." He stood and gave a little bow. "Welcome to the Lokelani."

Fatinah returned home to find her husband drinking his tea. His eyes were tired, but aware.

"Where have you been, love?"

"It is good to see you up. How do you feel?"

He lifted his amputated arm. "It's strange. Aches like the arm is still there. But my head feels clearer. How long until I'm able to work, do you think?"

She hesitated, wondering how much to tell him. "It's going to take some time for you to gain your strength. Elder Koru said we may find something to help your recovery at Aloka-pasar. It's an island market. I've already booked us passage."

Hasahn grinned. "Anything to get me back on my feet faster. When do we leave?"

"We're going to the ship tonight. I promised them the rest of your boar for passage. We feast with them, then set sail in the morning."

"Good, good. Come here." He set his mug down and patted the bed beside him. She snuggled up next to him as he put his good arm around her. Soon she would have to get up, eat something. And find some help to haul the meat to the ship, and then pack some things for the trip. A clean pair of clothes, some food, anything she could use to barter at the market—local tea leaves, a few pieces of jewelry, and a few coins she had found washed ashore when she played on the beach as a child. Hopefully, they didn't only accept coin, like the mainland was rumored to. But that was later. For now, she was safe beside her husband. Home. She would enjoy this moment while it lasted.

Hasahn suggested Pali for an extra set of hands for Fatinah's errands. The boy was glad to help. Pali had never set foot on a merchant ship, just the small fishing vessels. He was always eager to learn and quickly shadowed the sailors, asking them about their work. Fatinah assured him he could ask more questions later, after he carried her packs and the basket of meat. The two of them helped Hasahn onto the ship. His energy drained quickly. The cabin Tanroa assigned to them was small, with two hammocks bolted into the walls and a single chest. The chest was still plenty big enough for the few belongings Fatinah had packed. Pali helped her lower Hasahn into one hammock, and he quickly drifted off to sleep from the effort of getting there. She hoped he would sleep most of the journey. Maybe she could even get a draught from Elder Koru to help with that, so he wouldn't realize how sick he still was.

Elder Koru was happy to help, and warned her to watch for fever, and how to care for him as the venom spread.

The storm hit just as they were preparing supper. The ship rocked despite its anchor, and Fatinah's stomach dropped. She wasn't sure how much she would eat tonight. The mess hall was decorated with lanterns and the sailors ignored the rocking ship as they sang and drank and ate seasoned boar and fish and melons. Having noticed Pali's interest in the ship and sailing, the captain had invited him to stay for supper. Pali drank some of whatever the sailors were having and quickly passed out in a corner. One sailor draped a blanket over him. Fatinah could not eat between the rocking of the ship and worry over her husband. Once she felt it polite enough, she excused herself to go back to her cabin. Curling up in the opposite hammock, she let the ship rock her to sleep.

Fatinah woke to shouts and the thudding of footsteps on the ship. It sounded like their voyage had begun. She fumbled for the shutters on the porthole and opened it for a blast of fresh, salty air. Hasahn woke long enough to use a bucket to relieve himself and drink from the flask of medicine Elder Koru prescribed. She offered him some bread, but he mumbled something incoherent, waving his stump of an arm, then slumped back to the hammock. His skin was warm, but not overly hot. Fatinah peeled back the cloth on the stump and hissed. The skin was hotter here, definitely inflamed, and the black veins were stronger, creeping further.

Fatinah made use of the bucket herself, then took it out to empty it over the side of the ship. After skipping dinner the night before, she was starving. Thankfully, there was porridge in the mess hall. The crew was more friendly than when she had first boarded, greeting her with nods and waves.

The sky was clear this morning, with a brisk breeze perfect for the sails. She hoped for good time. She heard familiar laughter and turned to find Pali looking out over the edge of the ship, the wind blowing through his uncombed hair.

"Pali! Why are you still here?"

"The sailors didn't want to wake me. And I figure you could use my help, what with Hasahn being unwell and all."

"But I didn't pay for your passage."

The boy shrugged. "The crew likes me. I've been helping out around the ship, learning the ropes. Don't you worry for me."

There was no turning the ship around at any case. Fatinah convinced herself it would be fine. She'd have to apologize to Pali's parents later for inadvertently kidnapping the boy.

Captain Tanroa was in his cabin this morning, poring over the maps. He pointed out their path for the day, stopping at two smaller islands before reaching Aloka-pasar.

The first of the islands was similar in size to her island home of Kalana. The crew did a quick stop, efficiently trading goods on and off the ship, before moving on.

They reached the second island while the sun was high, and Tanroa encouraged Fatinah to walk off her sea legs. Fatinah woke Hasahn and managed to get him up and moving with her. He was sluggish, no surprise between the medicine and the sickness, but she hoped the walk and air would do him good. He kept his good arm around her for support while they walked the docks. This island was flatter than Kalana. It appeared to be mainly a fishing village, with terraced plots of rice. A local family offered to feed them, serving fish on rice, with a subtle seasoning. Hasahn ate some of the rice, but ignored the fish.

When they returned to the cabin, Hasahn focused on Fatinah and kissed her. "You are so good to me. I hope I regain my strength soon so I can take care of you."

"Of course, Love. Now rest. Next stop is our destination. We'll get you healed in no time." She hoped he couldn't see the worry in her eyes in the dim light.

Knowing she would need energy to disembark once they arrived at the market, Fatinah napped as well. It was a restless sleep. Mostly, she looked across the room and watched her husband. If the hammocks were bigger, she would have climbed in beside him. She missed his strength. She had to be the strong one now. Eventually the sound of the waves soothed her to sleep, as she awoke to pounding on her door.

"Port ahead! Prepare to disembark."

Fatinah climbed out of the hammock and leaned over to wake Hasahn. He was noticeably warmer and wouldn't rouse. Fatinah went up deck for help, but the crew was busy with sail and rope and positioning the boat at the dock. She found Pali and asked him to carry their bags, while she found stronger arms to help Hasahn.

At the previous docks, the Lokelani had been the only merchant ship. Here were more than a dozen boats; from one person craft, to large three masted ships that towered over the rest, the docks stretched as far down the coast as she could see. At least with so many ships she should be able to find one returning down–island when they were ready to return home. She would have to deal with that when the time came.

Everywhere she looked were wooden buildings, up the cliffs, down the coast, stacked atop each other. The market was the island, winding around soil and rock. She saw no farms, no jungle for hunting, barely even a sight of fishing boats. Most food must be imported.

She dragged her gaze from the overwhelming sight and grabbed a passing sailor. "Could you help me? My husband is ill and won't wake."

"Plenty of porters just ashore."

"Porters?"

He gestured to a shack with men sitting around it, smoking and chatting. "Men for hire. They can help with your things, and also give direction."

The porters were eager to help, jumping to their feet at her approach. She chose a lad that was tall and wide, sturdy enough to support her husband if they still could not wake him. She offered an heirloom pearl necklace as payment.

"Me name is Daki. I show you a place to stay. Then you show me what needs carrying."

Daki introduced her to a nearby inn, a multi-layered building jutting out from the cliff where she arranged for a small room for the price of the few coins she happened to have. Daki was able to wake Hasahn to partial consciousness and half-carried him to the room. Pali followed with their bags, having brought nothing of his own but the clothes on his back. "Find me again if you need more help," Daki said. "That is a fine payment that will cover multiple jobs."

"Thank you, Daki."

Hasahn's fever was worse. Fatinah ordered broth from the kitchen to keep him hydrated, and a bucket of rags and water to cool him. Pali ended up being a fine helper, making sure Fatinah ate some food as well. Pali slept on the floor while Hasahn took the small bed. Fatinah lay next to her husband, but slept fitfully.

It was a long night, and Hasahn's fever did not break. The black veins were clearly visible above the bandage, inching toward his shoulder, ever closer to his heart. Only two more days to save him.

Pali saved her from having to find help to watch Hasahn. She didn't dare leave him alone, as sick as he was. Fatinah showed Pali how to help Hasahn sip broth and when to use blankets or cool rags. There was no more need for the sleeping draught. Fatinah worried if he fell into a deep enough sleep now that he wouldn't wake. She kissed his fevered forehead and took her bargaining bag into the market.

First, she sought a healer. There must be one in a city this big. A man in blue robes welcomed her into his shop, what he called an apothecary. Shelves of colored bottles and dried herbs lined the walls. She described the sun viper bite and her husband's symptoms. The man shook his head. There was nothing he could do at this stage. No traditional healer could help.

Stalls bustled with life and possibility. You could find anything here in Aloka-pasar. Macabre displays of bone and feather and fur. Dolls with animal heads. Plants with teeth. Dangling bead and bone curtains. Glass globes and lanterns filled with plants. Some sort of animal fetus in a jar. A bat skeleton. Even a turtle with two heads. Sculptures of wood and bone and iron. Eyeballs and tentacles. Life and death coexisting.

And the smells, overwhelming that of the salty sea. Cinnamon, pastry, unknown meats. Her stomach growled, but she moved on. She would not find what she needed in the food district.

Another healer sat in a tent of purple fabrics. She didn't have the trappings of the apothecary, or even of Elder Koru. Instead, she claimed the power of hypnosis and suggestion would cure all ills. Fatinah was sure that wouldn't help with snake venom.

A priest of the moon goddess Delwyn promised healing for any ailment, but only after an offering on the night of the full moon. The moon was only waning, so that would mean another three weeks of waiting; time Hasahn didn't have.

She found herbalists, midwives, shamans. None could help her. Weary from a day of rejection, she stopped at one of the food carts on her way back to the inn and comforted herself with a doughy cinnamon cake. For a few blessed moments, she was able to forget her dire mission and taste the buttery cinnamon sweetness that melted in her mouth. She wished she could share the treat with Hasahn. That thought brought her back to her reason for being there, and she hurried back for another miserable night. Praying to any gods that might hear that he would last the night and that she would find a cure for him tomorrow.

Six days since the snake bite. Hasahn's fever still raged. He woke when prodded, but didn't seem very coherent. Fatinah was grateful for Pali's help watching over him. Time was running out.

Hasahn refused to eat, but would at least drink a bit. Fatinah's stomach was too tied up to eat. If she didn't find a way to save her husband today, then she would stay by his side in his last hours.

Fatinah ventured deeper into the market. The people were getting as strange as the stalls. A woman passed her in a gray cloak and deer skull mask. A real snake curled around another woman's neck. Men and women alike sported black ink on their arms and faces. Some women went as shirtless as the men, draped in sheer fabrics. Children, too young for such a place, hid behind their mother's skirts, daring an occasional peek.

She besought help wherever she could, but no one knew of a cure for sun viper bite. Bumping shoulders with strangers, it was easy to get turned around, lose your sense of direction. She was no longer sure which way she came in or where she had been. Only that there was more market to see.

The sights blurred together. The sun beat down and enhanced the sweat and the pressure. Overwhelmed with sight and sound and smell, and not having eaten since the day before, she was losing herself. How would she find anything here? Where even was here? A whisper in her head like water, promising she was close. She just had to keep moving. Follow her desire. A path branched off into the blessed coolness of a rock overhang. Fatinah entered its shade and closed her eyes. The sound of water called her, not like the sea but bubbling water. She opened her eyes to see the overhang was actually the entrance to a tunnel. She focused on the sound and went further in, her hand trailing to follow the wall as, for a moment, everything was dark. Then the tunnel turned, and she saw a light. Blue and green fungus glowed, a trail leading her further in, until the passage opened into a glorious cavern. A natural spring bubbled up, the fungus glowing from under the water and above on the ceiling. It was magical.

A crackly voice came from the left. "Hello, there. Come, sit with me."

Fatinah turned toward the voice. An old woman had her gray hair woven into many braids. A deer skull mask hid her face. It could have been the same one Fatinah had passed earlier in the day. Her gray robe seemed to waver like smoke and Fatinah blinked to steady her vision.

"I have food. And tea. It looks like you could use some."

"Yes, yes. Thank you." Fatinah walked around the glowing pool to sit on a pile of pillows across from the cross-legged woman. The woman pushed a bowl of berries toward her, and Fatinah shoved a handful into her mouth, immediately feeling better. They were juicy and cool and sweet, bursting like bubbles in her mouth. The tea that followed grounded her, tasting like smoke and grass and earth.

"That tea will sharpen your senses." The woman placed a wrinkled hand on Fatinah's knee. "Only those in need may find this place. Tell me your woes, girl."

Unbidden, tears came to Fatinah's eyes. Her body ached and felt as if the weight of the world pressed upon her. She could feel the warmth of the woman's hand on her knee, and the brilliance of the fungus. Her story spilled out of her. "My husband. He is dying. He was bitten by a sun viper. The healer cut off his arm, but the venom had spread into his blood. We are running out of time, and no one can help. I'm going to lose him and be all alone. I don't know what to do. I had hoped... foolishly hoped that this island would have something more. A way to save him."

The woman moved to kneel directly in front of Fatinah, placing her hands on the sides of Fatinah's face. "Your hope is not in vain. I know of a way not only to cure him, but to make him whole again. There is a ritual."

"Oh yes. Anything. Thank you, thank you. What do I need to do?"

The woman gave her a list of things to procure. Instructed her on how to set up the ritual and the words to say.

"I have so little left. How can I afford all this? And how will I ever pay you? What is your name and how will I find you again?"

"I am unimportant. I do not require your coin or your gratitude. Your devotion is enough. That tea has opened your mind. Listen and let Shamanuc guide you and provide all that you need."

From what Fatinah had seen of the market, her list of items should be acquirable. Fatinah's focus heightened as she reentered the market. It seemed as if relevant items glowed: skulls a brilliant white, glass shimmering and calling to her. Had the tea done this? What had been in it? And who was Shamanuc? That and the other names in the ritual sounded familiar, but when she tried to focus on them the memories slipped away. Her thoughts kept returning to her list of items: a small animal skull, a glass bowl, sea salt, seeds of the cusklo flower, a sharp knife, and a full-length mirror.

She found the glass bowl first, wider than her cupped hands, tinted blue like the sea. The other items would rest nicely inside, except for the mirror, of course. A small animal skull. The booth with the bat skeleton had additional, unattached bat skulls, perfect size. She stopped for a moment on her way to look for the next item. The bat skull sat in the bowl, so she definitely acquired those. But she didn't remember bartering for them at all. Her bartering bag still had everything she'd started the day with. Shamanuc must have provided as promised. She would trust the process.

She followed her nose to the food district. Plenty of vendors sold seasoning and spices such as the sea salt. A small pouch of sea salt was probably more than enough. The same stall had an obsidian knife. Down to the seeds and the mirror. Cusklo flowers were like bell lanterns. They grew on the cliffs of her own island. The seasoning vendor said the seeds were decorative rather than edible, and would unlikely be sold at the market, but that they did grow here. Whispers called to her, and she closed her eyes to focus on them. The woman had said Shamanuc would lead her.

The words, if they were words, didn't translate for her, though she sensed where they were leading her. She opened her eyes and one path through the market was lit, as if her peripheral vision had lost color. She followed the path, leading further inland. The wooden planks of the path ended at a steep, rocky path up the cliff. Cusklo flowers dangled down over the edge. She would have to pick them herself. She set her bowl and her bag at the base of the cliff. There were handholds carved into the rock beside the steep path, allowing her to at least brace herself as her feet slid on loose stones. A few times she slipped and bit her tongue with fear she would tumble all the way down. Her hands grew raw from gripping the rock. Finally at the top, she hauled herself over the last ledge and lay on her back for a moment, shaking her stinging hands.

This was merely another ledge before another cliff. But there were flowers here. All dangling over the edge of the cliff she had climbed. She raised the stems, inspecting for the fruit of the flowers. One cluster had just seeded, the orange hard center in a lace-like papery pod. Six seeds. That should be enough. To keep her hands free on the climb back down, she bit the stem in her mouth. It tasted bitter. Hopefully, it wasn't as toxic as the seeds.

Down was much quicker, but no less heart racing. Her feet practically slid down the slope and she scraped her hands more while slowing her descent. Back at the bottom, she delicately twisted the seed pods off their stems and added them to the glass bowl. She looked at her red scraped palms. This wouldn't do. She still had some of the ointment for Hasahn's wound in her bag. When she rubbed it on her hand, there was a momentary sting, but then it numbed them. She tore strips off her skirt and wrapped them around her hands.

She checked her purchases. Skull, bowl, salt, seeds, knife. Just the mirror to go.

So close. She didn't know if the words were her own. Back into the market, each piece of glass shone out at her from within the stalls. When she caught her own reflection, she would stop and ask about the mirror. Most were too small.

She turned a corner and was dazzled by an entire stall of mirrors. Some hanging from the ceiling, some propped on counters. And one exquisite mirror propped in the center. Her own reflection looked back at her, her simple round face, lank dark hair, blouse stained with dirt and sweat, and torn skirt. *This is it,* the voice whispered. *The mirror needed to complete the ritual. Save your husband.* Before she couldn't understand the words, but this came through clearly. Perhaps because she was so close, in front of the last item.

The seller said something, but she didn't hear the words. The mirror drew her. She reached out to touch the frame. The wood was carved with symbols and painted gold. Never had she seen something so rich, so gaudy, yet she had to have it. For the ritual. The price was high. She was willing to barter all she had left, knowing it couldn't possibly be enough, yet the vendor waved her bag away, said it was already paid for, and asked where to deliver it. Fatinah named the inn she was staying at. Where Hasahn waited for her. The shopkeeper provided a porter to carry the mirror, wrapped in a blanket, and Fatinah led him back to her room, clutching the bowl of ritual ingredients before her.

Hasahn had worsened through the day. Fatinah returned to find him thrashing and muttering incomprehensibly. The blanket had been thrown to the floor.

Pali huddled in the corner on a stool. "I'm sorry. I don't know how to help him. He just keeps shaking. He knocks me back if I try to feed him." An empty bowl sat in a puddle near the head of the bed. "He's not going to get better, is he."

Fatinah put a reassuring hand on the boy's shoulder. "It is fine. You did your best. I couldn't do this without you. And I found a way to help him." She dug out her other piece of jewelry, a carved wooden band that Hasahn had whittled. "You've been stuck in this room for too long. You could use some fresh air. Take this to the food market. Get yourself a treat. They have some delicious cinnamon cakes."

Pali hesitantly looked at Hasahn, then nodded, grabbed the bracelet, and dashed out of the room.

The porter propped up the mirror across from the bed, turned to reflect her poor husband. Then he hurried out as well, probably worried her husband had some contagious disease.

Fatinah put her hands on Hasahn's shoulder. "Shh, I'm here, my love. You're going to be okay."

He calmed. "Fatinah... it hurts... make it stop." His eyes looked toward her but were clouded. The veining on what remained of his arm had reached his shoulder.

She prayed this ritual would work. They didn't have the time to find any other solutions. She kissed him, his lips hot against hers. "Soon."

The room was small, the only furnishings were the bed, the stool, and a dresser. No desk or table. The stool Pali had sat on would have to do. Fatinah set it between the bed and mirror. She spread the blanket on the floor nearby to set her ingredients in easy reach. "Bowl, skull, salt, seeds, knife, mirror," she muttered to herself.

She centered the blue glass bowl on the stool. The bat skull went in the center. She sprinkled sea salt around it. Then she cupped the delicate cusklo seeds and parted her hands to let them drop into the bowl.

"Look into the mirror, Hasahn." Fatinah stepped to the side so she could reach over the bowl without blocking his view. She took the knife. He had suffered so much pain. It was time for her to return the favor. She held up her hand and bit her lip to keep from crying out as she dug the knife into the fatty part of her palm. The blood dripped, painting the bat skull. The seeds and salt soaked up her blood.

Now for the words. Earlier her focus was on the ingredients, not the words of the ritual. When she tried to remember in the market, she knew they were there, waiting, but she couldn't recall them exactly. She could hear them now, whispering as a reminder, her inner voice or something more. "Mahallaliel, Kabarac, Great Ones of the Outer Isles, take the one before the glass, preserve them for all time, unless another is given; Shamanuc, Velekai, let it be done." Save him, she thought. Please. A dark mist came from the mirror. Fatinah dropped the knife, pressed her palm to stop its bleeding, and retreated until her back hit the wall. Was this Shamanuc? Coming out to save her husband?

Hasahn stared at the mirror and reached toward it with his remaining hand. Mist met fingers, entwined with them, and then... then he was gone. The mist was gone and her husband with it.

3

atinah screamed, "Hasahn!" The ritual was supposed to save him. Where did he go?

"I'm here, love."

She could hear him. Why couldn't she see him?

"I... I think I may be in the mirror. Looking out, I can see a room, a bed. Vaguely familiar."

Fatinah hesitantly stepped back in view of the mirror. And instead of her reflection looking back, there he was. She reached out, put her hands on the glass. "Hasahn? You can hear me? What happened?"

"Yes, I hear you. I see you." He placed his right hand against hers, but all she felt was the cold surface of the mirror. "The last few days were such a blur. I felt I was losing myself. Drifting further from this life. But now... now my mind is clear. And look!" He held up the stump of his left arm. "It doesn't hurt anymore."

The black veining was gone, as was the redness. His arm remained amputated, but looked healthy. "So it worked? We saved you? But you're trapped."

"But we can see and speak. I am alive and here. If this is my fate, to be trapped in a mirror, at least I will still be by your side."

"I... I suppose." He wasn't dead. That is what she had asked for. With the ritual done, and the efforts of the day, she suddenly felt drained. Her awareness dulled to normal, her knees weakened. Her body felt so heavy again.

"You look tired. Sleep, love. And I will watch over you."

Yes, sleep. So tired. Whatever had been in that tea must have worn off. She sank down to the bed and watched her husband in the mirror until she sank into darkness.

The morning sun woke her. Rubbing her eyes, she sat up and suddenly remembered. She looked at the mirror and only saw herself. "Hasahn!"

The mirror transformed into swirling fog, replacing her image with his. She breathed easily again. "I thought I lost you."

"I'm here. I heard you call for me."

A strangled gasp came from below. Pali! She had forgotten about the boy.

Pali sat up from his blanket on the floor and skittered backward, eyes on the mirror. "I thought... I came back and you were sleeping. And Hasahn was gone. I thought... I hoped he was better. Out at the market. But... but... he's in the mirror. What is going on?"

Fatinah rubbed her face. "I wish I had a good answer. The bite is healed. Hasahn is no longer dying. But, for now at least, he is in the mirror. Safe and alive." She hoped. "Why don't you go downstairs and get us some breakfast?"

"Is it really you, Hasahn?" Pali asked.

"Yes, it's me. Thank you, Pali, for watching over me."

"And... do you need food, too?"

Hasahn frowned for a moment. "No. I don't believe I do. I don't feel hunger, or fatigue." He smiled. "I haven't felt this well in some time. Now go, do as Fatinah asked."

Pali nodded and backed out the door, keeping his eye on the mirror until he was out of the room.

Fatinah turned her attention back to her husband. "What is it like in there?"

He shrugged. "Nothing solid. Like the fog rolling in from the sea. I walked for a bit into it, but found nothing. I thought of you, and I was in front of the glass again, watching you sleep."

That sounded terribly boring. "So, you just watched me sleep all night?"

His eyes lit up. "Oh no. This glass is wondrous. I thought of home, and I saw it! Like I was there in our hut. It's like a scrying pool. It shows me any place or thing I think of. I'm not trapped at all; I have the entire world at my fingertips."

"Coming back to me... that pulled you from a new adventure?"

"I will always come at your call. You are mine and I am yours."

Fatinah ventured once more into the market. She intended to find the old woman again. The ritual had worked, yes. As intended? She didn't know. Certainly not as Fatinah had expected. She considered her words as she wound deeper into the market. What would she say to the woman? Thank her or curse her? Hasahn was saved. Hasahn was trapped. Was this a blessing or a curse? Only time would tell. She hoped the woman would have answers at least. Fatinah should have asked more questions.

But she hadn't been thinking clearly. Perhaps it was the tea. Or merely her desperation.

Briefly she stopped at the mirror booth, spoke her husband's name in one mirror. Nothing happened. So, he wasn't trapped in all mirrors. Only hers.

She asked around with the one name she remembered, Shamanuc; most claimed not to know what that meant. A few, like the priest of Delwyn, completely closed off the conversation at the name and refused to speak more to her.

The cavern eluded her. No one she talked to knew how to get there. Had she imagined it? There had been a cavern. And a woman. She wouldn't have known the ritual on her own. Something had led her. And now... now she couldn't find her way back. The woman's words came back to her. *"Only those in need may find this place."* Fatinah's wish had been granted. Her need done. The cavern gone.

Eventually, she gave up and found her way back to the inn. Pali had returned as well and was chatting more comfortably with Hasahn. Fatinah asked her husband to leave their view. She would call him back when they were safely home. She didn't want anyone seeing him, asking questions. The mist covered him, and she was alone with her reflection. All she could see was the fatigue and stress emanating from herself. She much preferred looking at Hasahn. She tossed the extra blanket over the mirror and went to find passage home.

With so many more ships at this port, it was easier than Fatinah expected to find one traveling back toward Kalana. When the captain asked about payment, Fatinah looked through her nearly full barter bag. She had no more need of the medicines Elder Koru had provided. The rest of the sleeping draught, the ointment, along with some teas. The captain accepted what she offered.

"I can't afford to offer you a cabin, but you can ride in the cargo hold."

Daki, the porter that had helped her before, offered his services again as she approached. He made conversation as they returned to the inn. "How is your husband?"

"He... he didn't make it. I have little to carry. You will see."

She showed him the mirror. It was too big for her or Pali to carry. He gave her a quizzical look. "It was... a gift. All I have left to remind me of my husband. I just have that and my bag of clothing." She had kept the knife and bowl tucked in her clothing bag. The other components had simply vanished, along with the blood.

"Of course. I'm sorry. Let's get this on board for you."

Thus, she returned home with her husband in a mirror.

Fatinah regrettably had to get help to move the mirror again once the ship docked at Kalana. Between that and Pali's chatter, it was impossible to keep the secret of her new mirror from the village. The first few days she had many visitors wanting to see this strange new artifact. Many of the villagers didn't have a normal mirror, let alone a magical one. Hasahn humored them, showed them things they asked. Thankfully the village settled back into normalcy before long.

In the mornings, Fatinah found work where she could. Though the village would always provide for a widow—which she technically was, with her husband no longer present to provide for her—Fatinah was still young and wanted to keep her hands busy. She shucked oysters, and often went into the jungle gathering flowers and such for pigment, and finding herbs for Elder Koru. Their neighbors—Pali, his parents, and two sisters—insisted that she join them for meals. Then she would spend her evenings with Hasahn, talking of her day, sharing memories, and learning what Hasahn had seen. Fatinah could even see some images as well, but only if she spoke the desire, it had to come from her and not merely Hasahn telling her. She preferred listening to Hasahn's tales though, as she got to watch his animated face, imagine he was fully in the room with her, as they related how they each spent their day.

The villagers mostly respected her privacy, but she knew Pali would often sneak in to speak to Hasahn and see the wonders of the world with him.

Hasahn still had most of his days and nights alone with the scrying mirror. He had always wanted to see the world. But few leave their island homes. And he had Fatinah. He was a provider, not a sailor. Now he could spend an entire day following a pod of whales, or see the full breadth of the mainland. Sometimes he would find a person or family and follow their days, learn their story. Other times, he would hop from person to person in a busy town. Or avoid people altogether and be one with the boars.

When his arm was first cut off, right at the elbow joint, he could still feel it there. But now, he saw, his arm was longer. It was growing back. A miracle he would never have experienced out in the world. Though he had less use for it now, he felt more whole.

But as he was watching, he felt watched himself. At first, he thought it was merely the loneliness, and he called for Fatinah to wake her in the night to keep him company. Then after, in the silence before he called something to view in the glass, he felt prickles on his neck. He turned and shouted but could only see shadows around him. That endless mist. And then the whispers began. He wasn't sure if it was in the mists, or in his head. Gone when he tried to focus on them.

He even learned to sleep of sorts, to shut out the world and the mist and merely let time pass. He could see the world, but he wasn't truly a part of it. So many stories, but none of them his own. And then there was more than the mists. He wasn't sure how long he had been there in the mirror. He had nearly a full arm now. But it wasn't right. It wasn't his arm. It was darker somehow. And the whispers grew louder. He still couldn't understand them, but they seemed more present. More real. Shapes in the mist, gone when he turned to look at them fully.

Once, Hasahn woke from his false slumber, and his left arm twitched. Shadows had wrapped around it. He gasped and pulled it free. The stump... it was growing into something, but not a wrist and a hand like he had expected. It was thinner, wetter, darker. Tentacles splitting where there should be fingers. No, no. This wasn't him. He had to get out. The whispers were closer now, clearer, filling his head. He heard a name now. Shamanuc... Shamanuc. Hadn't that been in the ritual? What had been done to him?

He called for Fatinah, not caring what time it was. She appeared, sleeping in the darkness of their hut. "Fatinah!"

His wife shifted and opened her eyes. The mirror was propped to view most of the room, particularly the bed palette they had once shared. "Hasahn? What time is it? Is something wrong?"

"You have to get me out of here. Something is wrong. I'm not alone. I'm losing myself."

She quickly started a fire so she could see him clearly.

Hasahn lifted his deformed arm, the tentacles hitting the mirror with a splat, tiny suctions he couldn't see gripping the surface. "This isn't right!"

Fatinah stared at the mutated arm in horror. What was he becoming? What had she done to him? She had to find the woman, the witch, who did this. "You can see things. Can you find her? The old woman who did this? I don't know her name. But she was in a cavern with a pool, lit by glowing fungus. She wore gray robes and a deer skull mask."

"I can see so much. But I can't see her. If I try, all I see is darkness and my head hurts. I've seen every inch of that market and have never seen the cavern you spoke of."

Fatinah hadn't found the woman again back at the market. There was likely no chance she'd find her now if they returned to Aloka-pasar. They would have to do something themselves. "I'll talk to Elder Koru in the morning. Maybe he can help."

There was no way to ask Elder Koru for help without telling him the truth about Hasahn. Fatinah told him her story, of what she had seen and done at the market, and brought him to the mirror.

Elder Koru's face darkened. "I had heard the gossip, that Hasahn was somehow still living, but did not know you had turned to such a ritual. This is not good. And you say there was a name she told you?"

"Yes, she said Shamanuc would guide me."

Hasahn chimed in. "That's the same name I have been hearing as well."

Elder Koru sank onto a pillow. "I would not recommend saying his name again. It is an old tale. Many have forgotten. Have you heard of the Old Ones, the Old Gods?"

Fatinah leaned forward. "Of course. They rule the night, the sea, the shadows. Wait, that was part of the ritual. I didn't even realize what I was saying. The four names. The Great Ones of the Outer Isles."

"Yes. Old gods banished by those over the mainland. The Whisperer, The Trickster, The Underking, and The Drowned. That name you spoke; I believe he is The Whisperer. He was banished to the shadow realm. Which I fear is where you, Hasahn, are now trapped."

"I am sharing a space with a banished god?"

"And he is tainting you."

Fatinah moaned. "We have to get him out!"

"And if he reverts to his sickened state?"

Fatinah looked pleadingly at Hasahn, not sure how to answer.

Hasahn gestured to his left arm. "I would rather die than stay trapped here with this thing, transforming into... something else."

This was all her fault. She would have to fix it. "We'll repeat the ritual again, reverse it this time.

Elder Koru stood to leave. "If you resort to this ritual, I refuse to be a part of it. But it is your choice, it is not one I can make for you."

Fatinah squared her shoulders. "I have to try. I can't sit here and do nothing, when I'm the reason he's in this position. I'm sorry, Hasahn."

"Never be sorry for loving me."

Skull, bowl, sea salt, seeds, knife, mirror.

Fatinah still had the mirror, of course. She set out the bowl and the knife. She still had some sea salt. The seeds she would have to harvest herself. The cusklo flowers grew near cliffs; she had seen some while she gathered for Elder Koru. She took a basket and entered the jungle, staying out of the shadows where any snakes might be sleeping. She did not want to replicate Hasahn's condition. Being well fed, clear of mind, and familiar with the island, the task was easier than on Aloka-pasar. She still felt the memories of those scrapes on her hands while she harvested the seed pods. Memory takes much longer to heal than skin.

Pali would often go with her on her foraging, eager to learn from everyone and everything. The boy brought home anything that caught his eye. Strange stones, colorful shells, and even the occasional animal skull. Fatinah perused his collection and traded for a snake skull. It seemed most fitting.

That evening, she prepared for the ritual a second time. The night was cool, so she wore a cloak.

Hasahn watched her from within the glass, face pale and eyes haunted.

Fatinah kissed her fingertips and pressed them onto the mirror. "I will fix this, Hasahn."

In response, he placed his two hands against the mirror, the one healthy and whole, the left crude and tentacled. His eyes grew hungry. She had to get him out of there.

She knelt on the floor this time, the bowl before her. She placed the snake skull, sea salt, and seeds. Traced the scar on her palm from the last time she had done this.

She had thought to save him. First from the fate of death, now from the madness of the mirror. How many ways could she lose him? If this didn't work... She shook her head. No use thinking like that. The knife slid over her skin easily, and she spoke the words. They were like a prayer, a mantra. It was hard to remember the phrases in the daylight; the memory slipping out of her grasp like fog, but they slithered out of her with ease as she did the ritual, almost as if the words weren't her own. She thought to reverse the phrasing, to reverse the spell. But once the words began, once she named the great ones, the words continued on their own. She could not stop them.

"Mahallaliel, Kabarac, Great Ones of the Outer Isles, take the one before the glass, preserve them for all time, unless another is given; Shamanuc, Velekai, let it be done."

The words spoken, she scrambled to the side, hoping to avoid the mists as they emerged from the mirror. They still found her. Consumed her.

Once the shadows cleared, she could see Hasahn standing in their hut, looking at the mirror. Looking, she realized, at her. No, no. This wasn't supposed to happen. She pounded her fists on the glass. "Hasahn! You're free. Are you still..."

He lifted his left hand, the tentacled one. "Thank you, Fatinah. I could not have escaped without your aid."

"Find the priestess, or acolyte, or whoever she is."

He nodded. "Now rest."

With that command, Fatinah blacked out. When she awoke, she was alone. The hut was empty. But was she alone in here, in this realm of shadows? She turned, pressing her back to the mirror glass, and scanned around her. Mists, shadowed emptiness. "Hello? Is anyone there?" Silence greeted her. She waited there, for an unknown stretch of time, waiting for Hasahn to call her back. Or for whispers from the shadows. But there was nothing. Perhaps Hasahn had merely gone crazy in his time trapped here. Or the entity in the mirror world was gone.

4

Fatinah did not tire, nor hunger as time passed within the mirror. But her soul tired, her heart hungered. She stared into the unending nothingness. The swirling fogs that muffled even her inner thoughts. Her cloak did nothing to protect from the chill. She had done this to Hasahn. Trapped him here. Why had she ever listened to that woman in the market? She could blame it on the tea, the hunger, on not being in her right mind. But she knew, deep down, that it was her own fear and desperation that had led them there. If she had only let him go, he would be in the sea's embrace now. And she... she would be alone. But not truly. Not as she is now. She would have had Pali, her other neighbors, Elder Koru. The village would have supported her.

Hasahn had said the mirror could be used to scry. Hasahn had not called her, but she should be able to see him. Fatinah turned her back on the emptiness and touched the rectangle of glass. It seemed to float. If she looked around it, there was more mist on the other side. "Show me Hasahn."

Darkness swirled in the mirror, revealing Hasahn on the docks. He chatted with the sailors. A long cloak hid his malformed arm. The men laughed at something her husband said. She focused further on listening in. Hasahn spoke again, but it was muffled. Like the mirror filtered out his words somehow.

Though she couldn't hear his words, they caused shivers up her neck. The cadence reminded her not of the way Hasahn would speak, but of the half-heard whispers she had heard before.

That evening he went out with the fishers. She urged the mirror to follow, but felt herself pulled back to the hut.

"Fatinah! Are you here?"

Elder Koru! "I'm here! In... in the mirror."

Elder Koru stepped in front of her view. His eyes were dark and haggard. "What happened, my daughter?"

Fatinah pressed her forehead to the glass and sighed. "I tried the ritual again. I don't know why I expected something different. Something better. Now I am the one trapped. But I kept my promise. Hasahn is healthy and free. He can live his life, see the world."

"That's why I came to find you. Hasahn is not the same man he was."

"Perhaps it was simply trauma from being sick and then trapped? He needs time for his mind to heal."

"Oh, he is not acting traumatized at all. And it has already been a week."

"A week?" So much time had passed in the nothing. It had felt more like a long day. "Why didn't you come sooner?"

"I tried. Hasahn wouldn't let me speak to you. This is the first he has let the hut out of his sight. He said you found a way to free him, but it left you fatigued, overwhelmed, and that you needed rest. This morning Pali offered to bring you his mother's soup, and Hasahn growled at him, knocked the soup into Pali's face, burning him."

Pali had been like a son to her. So sweet. Hasahn had always been generous and kind. This was nothing like him. "Will Pali be okay?"

"I have him resting in my hut. I fear he may lose sight in one of his eyes. But he will live. Has Hasahn spoken at all to you?"

Fatinah shook her head. "Not since thanking me for setting him free. I kept hoping... I called him every night. And now... now it's been a week, and he hasn't called for me. And now to hear of this... What if... What if it's not him? What if he was right, and there was something in here with him? And now... Now it's out."

"Maybe it's contamination from that arm. Maybe it's not too late. If we cut it off, perhaps we will free him from whatever influence is over him."

"I doubt he will let you cut off his arm again."

"I will drug him and do it while he sleeps."

Elder Koru left to get supplies and returned with sleeping powder. They didn't know what Hasahn would eat, so he put it in the water barrel instead, and some more in with the embers of their fire. "I will return after dark."

Once Elder Koru left, Fatinah used the mirror to scry for her husband again. His boat was just pulling into the dock. The two fishermen he had left with were nowhere to be seen, but the baskets were filled with fish. He left the boat unmoored and took the fish back to the hut.

Fatinah pounded on the mirror. "Hasahn!" He didn't look her way. Without being called, all on his side was just a reflection. He couldn't see or hear her. Still, he didn't call. He tossed his cloak aside, his left arm still purplish tentacled. Using the tentacle, he braced the fish while he gutted it with a knife in his other hand. Then put it on a spit over the fire. The smoke should be filled with sleeping dust. If he didn't breathe it in, it should at least infuse the fish. He ate before the mirror, a smirk on his lips. Was it just her imagination, or were his teeth sharper? Still, he didn't call her. Having eaten, he tossed the fish bones into the crackling fire and went to bed. Not sprawled face down like he used to, but flat on his back, eyes closed, more like a corpse than a man.

A short time later, Elder Koru sneaked in, the knife in his hands glinting in the remains of the fire. Hasahn's deformed arm lay in easy access beside him. Elder Koru raised the knife above the arm.

Hasahn's eyes remained closed, the rest of him unmoving, yet the tentacle shot up and wrapped around Elder Koru's neck. Squeezing, squeezing. No amount of hollering or pounding from Fatinah could stop anything. Elder Koru dropped the knife and tried to remove the tentacle, but it closed tighter. His face grew purple, his eyes went red. Gurgling horribly at first, then utterly silent struggles. Until he grew limp and the tentacle released him. A terrible smile crept onto Hasahn's face as he supposedly continued to sleep.

Fatinah couldn't breathe. Elder Koru was dead. And Hasahn—or whatever was using Hasahn—had killed him. She let the mirror grow dark as she turned away and dry heaved; any food in her body long since gone.

As the sun crept in that morning, Hasahn woke and packed a bag. Fatinah watched him roll Elder Koru's lifeless body in a blanket. He lifted the bundle as if it weighed nothing and carried it deep into the jungle. Fatinah saw predators prowling in the shadows and hoped they would take Hasahn down. But they ignored him as if he was one of their own. No, not one of their own, which they would fight for territory. But something greater, to be feared and avoided. Hasahn dumped Elder Koru in front of a den. He stepped back and watched, not hiding himself, as a large black cat padded out and sniffed the body.

She could swear the cat looked straight into Hasahn's eyes and nodded or bowed before it dragged the corpse back into its den.

Hasahn returned to the village, smiling and waving his good hand at his neighbors. He took his packed bag and left on the next boat. She didn't see him pay passage. She tried to overhear what he said to the captain, but again, his words were muffled to her. The captain's words came through clearly; the only one she couldn't understand was Hasahn.

Pali came to look for Fatinah, but found the hut empty. Fatinah could see him in front of the mirror, frowning and poking at his reflection. But he said nothing that might summon her. When Hasahn didn't return, the hut was emptied, and their belongings sold, including the mirror. No one in their small village had a need for such an extravagant thing. They didn't even use hand mirrors. She heard talk of using the money for someone to find a new healer, as Elder Koru had disappeared. It wasn't unusual for people to get lost to the jungle. Her husband was evidence of that. She had lost him that day he got bit by that snake. They never suspected murder. And if any had, well, the culprit was gone.

Fatinah may not be able to listen to Hasahn, but she watched her once husband. Watched as he did terrible things in the night. The ship he had ventured out on had a small crew, and they did not survive him. Each torn apart or sacrificed to the sea. His eyes turned black and hungry with each death. He took what he pleased and left no witnesses. She no longer saw the man she loved in him. Only the monster. Somehow, she would get out of this mirror, and she would hunt him down. Make things right again. She was the only witness to his crimes, the only one who knew the darkness that resided in him.

The mirror ended up back at Aloka-pasar, then bought by a mainlander along with other curiosities he thought would be of interest back at the mainland. Where a lovely noblewoman purchased it for herself.

"Mirror, mirror, I demand, who is the fairest in the land?"

And Fatinah was called to the mirror, compelled to answer truth.

Author's Note

This story has even less basis for a retelling, but is instead a prequel to *Mirror*. There are still fairytale elements such as a type of goblin market, bargains, rituals. This is also our first tale that takes place almost entirely outside of the mainland, and is not centered on nobility or royalty. Tales from the Outer Isles encompass my darker tales, not guaranteed to have a happy ending, and not under the watchful eyes of the Sky Gods and the muses. The Outer Isles are the dominion of the Old Gods. You won't find the muses stepping foot here.

I wanted the Tales from the Outer Isles to have a darker feel, with a dash of Lovecraftian horror. This was my first time writing darker fiction. I'm certainly no horror writer, but hope I at least created some chills.

Aloka-pasar is a mashup of Aloka (Malagasy for shadow) and pasar (Indonesian for market). It is literally a shadow market. A lot of the imagery was inspired by the Oddities and Curiosities Expo. It's a very strange place indeed.

Both Hasahn and Fatinah are Arabic names in origin. Hasahn means good, kind, and handsome. Which he certainly starts out as. But by the end he is no longer Hasahn. As mentioned in my Mirror notes, Fatinah means captivating or enchanting. She certainly becomes enchanted.

This is just one part of Fatinah's tale. I do plan to return to her for closure on her quest.

The Gloaming Realm

Mary W. Jensen

Contents

1

There once was a time when man did not rule this land. All of Tessagonia was a single kingdom, and Bentos and Delwyn lived among the people. The Sun God and Moon Goddess dwelt in a keep at the foot of the mountains, overlooking the Sea of Mystery. Here they raised their young daughters, encouraging them to explore their hobbies and desires as they discovered the facets that would someday define them as muses.

But all was not paradise on earth. As the eldest, Tesni, was on the cusp of adulthood, all seven sisters fell ill. The gods are not all-seeing, and alone could not discover the source of their daughters' condition. Thus Bentos sent out a proclamation, his voice booming across the land, echoing over mountain and vale, and rippling across the Sea of Mystery: Whosoever could save the seven girls, would gain the God's gratitude and receive a boon. Many came and failed to find cause or cure—scholars, warriors, and healers alike. To make matters worse, some of those investigating disappeared in the night. Did they flee from fear of retribution at their failure, or fall to a worse fate?

A modest incense farm rested in the keep's shadow. Close enough for Michael to hear Bentos bellow and banish those who tried and failed, and Delwyn wail as her daughters grew weaker. The sun continued to rise each day, but it felt hot and angry. Michael worried for the sake of his gardens and groves, but if men greater than him could not help, he knew not what an incense maker such as himself could do. As the days grew hotter and the nights colder, Michael hiked to the bank of the Sea of Mystery. He approached at twilight, the sky rich in purples, the air just cooling but still comfortable. Michael found a high rock to perch on and watch the churning water. He was hoping to create an irrigation system. His dull brown hair fell into his eyes as he speculated. Rumor was the water was enchanted. He had swum in the water just fine, but had never dared drink it. What would the water do to his crops? Perhaps it would be better to dig another well.

With the water hitting the rocks, he almost missed a secondary splashing. A dark shape twisted, coming closer to shore. Did something live in these waters? An arm broke through the sur-face, and another, a brief glimpse of a head, then flailing for a bit before disappearing again. Was someone drowning? Michael tugged off his boots and loose tunic, then dove into the water below. He swam out to the figure and put his arms around the slim body, pulling them both to shore. In the light of the full moon he could see it was a woman, hair and dress dark and drenched. He laid her on the rocky shore and leaned to check her breath. She coughed out water and sat up so abruptly that she hit her head on his.

Michael fell back, stars in his eyes. "Ouch. Sorry." He shook his head to clear it and looked closer at the woman. She was small, but mature. Possibly around his own age of twenty. Her eyes were pale, a silvery blue reflecting the light of the moon. "I... Are you well?"

She shook her head, leaned off to the side, and threw up; more than just water this time. After a bout of coughing, she raised a hand. "I think I'm good now. Thank you." Her voice was rough, though he couldn't tell if that was natural or from all the water she had coughed up. "I don't suppose you have something better than sea water to drink?"

Her face was angular and alluring. Her skin was pale, nearly to the point of translucence. Though, again, that could be due to nearly drowning. Michael caught himself and stood up, offering his hand. "I have tea back at the house. It's about a half-hour walk if you're up for it."

She took his hand and allowed him to help her to her feet. Which were dainty and bare. "I can manage that. Thank you."

He quickly fetched his shirt and put it on, grabbed his boots... "Did you want to wear my boots?"

"No, I'm used to the soil beneath my feet. Lead on."

Micheal shrugged, pulled on his boots, and led her back to his home.

The Kether cottage was a four-room house of sturdy sandalwood, built by Michael's father. His mother had started the gardens that surrounded it—one for flowers, one herb, and one vegetable. The sandalwood grove had been there for generations, but Michael was finding his own uses for the trees. Michael opened the door quietly, hoping not to wake his sisters.

The main room centered on the hearth, both kitchen and gathering space. The fire was down to embers. Michael gestured to the sitting area, and the woman chose a pile of pillows to collapse upon. Michael took a blanket from the rocking chair and tucked it around her shoulders.

After stoking the fire and heating some water, Michael also lit a sandalwood incense stick. He hoped the jasmine tea and the incense would calm her.

The tea he poured into clay mugs for both of them. The woman took hers and curled her whole body around it as she breathed it in before taking a sip. She let out a long sigh. "It's warm and sweet. I feel like I'm still outdoors. Thank you."

Michael gave her a moment to savor and warm herself before his curiosity got the better of him. "What happened tonight? Why were you in the water?"

She cringed. Perhaps he had overstepped. "I'm sorry, I shouldn't pry."

"No, it's fine. You have shown me much kindness this night. I lost someone close to me. And I ran away from home. I prefer to feel the earth beneath my feet, not to be suspended in water, but the path by water was less watched, so I tried to swim. So much water. Surrounding me. I am not a strong swimmer, and it felt as if the water wanted to hold me back. So, thank you. For saving me."

A door down the hall creaked, and they both turned toward the sound. "Mikey? Are you still up?" A small girl in a faded blue nightgown came into the room. Her blonde hair was mostly out of its braid.

Michael scooped her into his arms. "Did you have another bad dream?"

She nodded.

"Sit with us by the fire and share my tea."

"Us?"

Michael turned so the girl could see their company. "I realize we haven't shared introductions. I am Michael. This is my youngest sister, Daphne."

The woman waved. "Lovely to meet you, Daphne. My name is Halenka."

Daphne squirmed out of Michael's arms and scurried to sit in front of Halenka. "Would you fix my braid? My sisters are all sleeping, and Michael takes foreeever."

Halenka smiled. "Only if you'll do mine after." Michael handed Daphne the rest of his tea while he fetched a brush and some ribbons.

Daphne delighted in braiding Halenka's hair. Her technique was sloppy, but Halenka didn't seem to mind. As Daphne pulled back the rich brown strands, she gasped. "Your ears!"

Halenka's hand went up to one. "Are they hurt? Is something wrong with them?"

"No." Daphne pushed Halenka's hand back down. "They're pointy!"

Sure enough, her ears curved up into points.

"Oh, that." Halenka laughed. "That's because I'm a fae, silly."

Daphne's eyes went wide. "You mean you're... magic??" the last word whispered in awe. Faes were of the old tales told at bedtime. You certainly didn't expect one to wash up on your doorstep.

Halenka got a mischievous look and held up her palm. "Watch this." Tiny lights appeared above her fingers in myriad colors—yellow, blue, green, pink—which then fanned out to fill the room, some landing on Daphne's hair like a crown, making her giggle. They looked like tiny fireflies dancing through the air.

"What else can you do?"

"I can see auras."

"What's that?"

"It's a light that glows around a person or creature. Shows their true nature."

"What color is mine?"

Her head tilted as she examined Daphne for a moment, seeing what the others couldn't. "Pink. That means you are happy and kind. Which you have certainly been to me."

"Do Michael next!"

Halenka turned toward him. He could feel the intensity and energy radiating from her. "Blue. A protector of those around him."

She saw right through him, to the heart of things.

Halenka finally broke eye contact and poked Daphne. "I bet he takes good care of you."

Daphne giggled again. It warmed Michael to see her smile. He often wondered if he did a good enough job raising his younger sisters after their parents died. Halenka didn't know him well, or at all really, yet her validation mattered.

Daphne yawned. She shouldn't be up this late.

Michael scolded her. "Finish that braid so you can get back to bed."

The young girl caressed Halenka's locks. "Will you tell me a bedtime story? Michael never has any new ones, and I've never heard a *real* fae tale before."

Halenka glanced at Michael, who shook his head. "Not tonight," she said. Daphne drooped visibly. "I'll tell you one tomorrow."

The girl brightened back up. "You'll still be here in the morning?"

"I promise."

Daphne finished her rough braid of Halenka's hair, then insisted on the fae putting her to bed. Michael quietly showed her to the girls' bedroom. A bunk bed was built into each side wall. Nestled between them on the far wall was an enormous wardrobe.

While Halenka tucked Daphne into the empty bed, Michael rummaged through the wardrobe for a nightgown that should fit the fae.

Back in the kitchen, Michael handed Halenka the nightgown. "Something dry and warm for tonight." He refilled their mugs. "You're good with kids. Daphne already loves you."

"She is a gem. The feeling is mutual."

"If you're tired, you can sleep in my bed. We used to have a third bedroom, when my parents... Anyway, I converted it into a workshop. It's where I do my incense work."

"And where will you sleep?"

"On the floor in the workshop. I insist."

They both sat quietly for a bit, finishing their tea as the sparkling lights slowly dropped and faded. One last ember alighted on Halenka's cheek. Michael reached out and gently brushed it away. The light had little weight, floating away like a dandelion seed. Halenka's skin was soft and he let his fingers linger a moment longer. She flushed, and he pulled his hand away. "We should probably get some sleep."

She merely nodded.

Despite the late hour, Michael slept little, and was the first one up. He stoked the fire and made porridge for breakfast. His sisters shuffled in at various stages of awareness. Alissa, the eldest at sixteen, took after their mother the most with her red hair and green eyes. Saida and Amber got their father's dark looks. Six-year-old Daphne was the odd one, with her blonde hair and blue eyes.

Daphne's first course of action was to inquire after Halenka. Michael assured her she was here, but still sleeping. Daphne rambled throughout breakfast, telling her sisters about their fae guest. The older girls laughed and teased her, not believing her fantastical tale. A guest was rare enough; a magical one was inconceivable. Michael smiled to himself. They would meet her soon enough. The table took up half of the kitchen, still with empty chairs for their parents. It had been four years, but Michael still couldn't bear removing them.

Halenka wandered in as they were cleaning up their dishes. She looked like a ghost in her white nightgown, with her pale skin and eyes. She looked rested, at least.

"A story! You promised a story!" Daphne jumped up and down.

Michael pushed her back. "Why don't you all get dressed and ready for the day while our guest gets some food. Then we'll see about a story."

Daphne dashed down the hall. "And don't forget to brush your teeth!" Michael hollered after her. Michael introduced the other girls to Halenka as each passed her by returning to their room. They looked at her with curiosity, but Michael shooed them off.

Halenka took the bowl of porridge without complaint and sat at the table. "What happened to your parents?"

"Father died after a logging accident four years ago. My mother struggled to care for us without him, and she slowly wasted away. She practically stopped eating, prioritizing her children over herself. We had an unusually cold winter that year, and she didn't survive it."

"So, you raise these girls on your own?"

He nodded. "I do the best I can. I've grown my incense business, and we sell extra produce from the garden. But this summer has been hard on the crops. Bentos' rage at the plight of his daughters has caused a drought. I was considering irrigating with sea water when I saw you last night."

"Oh no. You shouldn't do that. Haven't you noticed the water is brackish? The salt would kill your crops."

"I... hadn't thought that through, I guess." He ran a hand through his hair.

Halenka stared into her porridge, stirring it without eating. "Bentos... he promised a boon. News of that has reached even the Gloaming Realm. If you helped him... it would stop the drought, and you could get help for your family."

Michael laughed. "Me, save the daughters of the gods? Not that I wouldn't want to. I would do anything to save my own sisters. I can't imagine what Bentos and Delwyn are going through. But me? What could I do?"

She licked her lips, then looked up to meet his gaze. "I could help. I... I don't know all of what is happening to them, but I know where the muses go each night."

Before Michael could get details, the girls were coming back in, Daphne in the lead, settling around the fire for a story.

"Do you mind?" He asked Halenka.

"I made a promise." She pushed away the rest of her porridge and sat in the rocking chair, the sisters looking expectantly up at her.

Michael washed the dishes while he listened to her tale.

There once was a young girl who loved to explore the woods. Each day, she would travel farther and farther. She would forage off mushrooms and berries, never paying attention to an actual meal time, just eating what she found when she found it. Her mother knew she was resourceful, simply chided her not to be out after dark, and to never, never talk to strangers. Strange things can happen in the woods at night. But one day the girl ventured so far, so deep, that she couldn't find her way back home before the shadows grew too dark.

The once welcome branches of the trees now seemed to loom and grab. Creatures howled and hooted, so different from the bright bird chatter of the day. And it being a warm day, she hadn't thought to bring her cloak. The night chill burrowed in her bones as she hurried back in what she hoped was the direction of home. Nothing looked the same, and as the hours passed, she worried if she was even traveling in the right direction.

Cold and frightened, she stumbled through the dark woods, scraping her arms on foliage she couldn't see until it was too late. Just as she was about to give up and stop for the night, she heard a new sound ahead. Music and laughter. She followed the joyous tunes, her heart lifting, until she broke through into a clearing.

A dozen figures wearing flowing clothes danced around a fire. Warmth and light and company.

One figure spotted her and approached. His face was narrow, his eyes bright, long dark hair fell past his shoulders. He smiled at her. Without a word, he lifted a hand and gestured her near.

The girl hesitated only a moment. Her mother had said not to talk to strangers, but no one was speaking. And she wanted to warm herself by the fire. She took his hand, and he led her to the group. Everyone laughed and smiled. After warming herself by the fire, surrounded by the dancers, one broke from the group again and approached her. This one held out a silver goblet. She hadn't realized until then how thirsty she was. The liquid smelled so sweet. She brought it to her lips and took a sip. Sparks ran through her, invigorating her. She felt so awake, so alive. She downed the rest of the nectar.

A girl her own age took her hands and pulled her into the dance. So the girl danced. And danced. And danced. They danced her all the way down into the Gloaming Realm. Where she continues to eat and drink and dance to this day. And that is why you must never go into the woods after dark, especially when Delwyn's gaze isn't watching over you.

Once the girls were off doing their chores, Michael and Halenka returned to their earlier conversation. "Is it true that you know something of the muses' ailment?" Michael asked. "You really think I'd have a chance at solving it?"

Halenka nodded. "The muses are drawn into the Gloaming Realm each night. If you could tell Bentos that, maybe he could stop it."

"Why don't you do it yourself? Save the day, claim the boon?"

Halenka dropped her chin, strands from her rough braid escaping to fall into her face. "I cannot. I am beholden to my king, unable to speak or act against him. And besides, your gods and mine don't exactly get along. I... fear that he wouldn't trust a fae."

"Your gods? Are Bentos and Delwyn not the only gods?"

"Of course not. The Old Ones of the Gloaming Realm, four siblings, have dwelt here long before Bentos' reign. I will not name them, for fear of drawing their notice. But they are not the benevolent beings you are used to."

"And you think they may be behind this?"

"I cannot say."

"Will you come with me at least? I only know what you've told me. I don't know if I could solve this without you."

Halenka sighed.

"I do have one other trick, which may help," Halenka said. "It requires a dark cloak, however. I had a lovely velvet one, but it didn't survive the swim."

Michael unearthed a faded brown cloak from his winter chest. It was heavy and warm rather than soft and elegant. "Will this do?"

Halenka held it up and shrugged. "It's not pretty, but it's functional." She slung it around her shoulders. Where the cloak hit him at the knees, it was ankle length on her more delicate figure. "Nice and long. And it has a clasp and a hood. It will do."

"So what will it do exactly?"

"It's hard to show when you're already being observed. But there's a fae trick to make oneself less visible. One doesn't disappear, but the eye glances over them like they aren't there. When your sisters return, I can show you."

"Today is market day, so they are in town bartering goods and running errands. I have errands of my own. The fish traps need checking."

"I will walk with you."

This morning's walk to the water was more pleasant than the previous night. There were three healthy size fish in the traps, so at least the drought hadn't affected the fish. Halenka refused to touch the fish. Michael simply laughed and put them in his basket.

Back at the house, Halenka helped Michael prepare some fish, rice, and vegetables to stew over the fire. Michael handled most of the work, while Halenka washed the rice and vegetables. Michael wondered what they ate in the Gloaming Realm. The pottage would feed his sisters until he got back in a few days. If he got back. No, he shouldn't think of any other possibility. He would return to his family. Not leave them without another parental figure.

Michael packed a backpack with things he might need for a stay at the keep—an extra set of clothes, loose incense to calm his nerves, a portable incense burner, and his notebook and inks.

They had just finished a light lunch of bread and cheese when they heard the girls. The sisters were noisy as ever as they chatted, coming down the lane to the house. Halenka quickly pulled the hood over her face and moved into a shadowed corner, sinking in on herself like she was going to shrink into the wall.

Saida and Amber continued their gossip they overheard in town, ignoring both Michael and Halenka. That proved nothing other than they were young girls. Alissa took everyone's baskets from the market and began moving things to the cupboards and pantry. Daphne, however, pranced in, dropped her bag of vegetables on the table, then approached Michael, where he sat before the fire. "Where's the fae? Did she go home already? I wanted another story!"

Michael shrugged in response. "She should still be here somewhere." The fae in question was standing in arms' reach to Daphne's right. Halenka even took a step closer.

Daphne pouted and looked around. "I'll check the bedrooms. Halenka!" she hollered as she dashed to the back of the house.

Halenka removed her hood. "Well?"

Alissa dropped the bag of flour she had been holding and turned with a jump. "How long have you been standing there?"

A handy trick indeed. Michael asked Halenka, "Can you come with me to the keep like that?"

"It works better in the dark. If you insist on my being there, I can meet you after sundown. I can get past the guards; meet me at the servants' entrance to the kitchen."

"You know the keep's layout?"

"No. But my nose can always find a kitchen."

2

The Keep of the Sky Gods sat at the foot of the mountains, on a cliff overlooking the inland sea. The stone walls had a subtle glow at night, like that of the moon itself. In the daylight, the sun reflected off the stone. A path wound up the cliff from the village below to the gap in the cliff-side that was breached by a curved bridge in the same stone as the keep.

Michael approached the grand keep. He had lived in its shadow, but never been so near. And to intend to impose on the gods, enter their home... he felt unnerved. He chided himself. He was here to help, not seek something for himself. Inhaling deeply, he adjusted his pack strap before making his way over the bridge and towards the gates. One of the two guards waved him forward. What would it be like to serve a god? With his nerves and wandering mind, he almost missed the guard's question.

"Do you seek an audience with Bentos?"

"I do. Regarding his daughters' plight."

"Many have walked that path and failed. Most haven't been seen since setting foot inside these walls. Even our regular petitioners have stopped coming. Do you still wish to proceed?"

So the rumors were true. People were disappearing. Michael glanced back the way he had come. He couldn't see Halenka, but he pictured her face, remembered her words. If she was right, and he could solve this, then it was worth the risk. "Yes. I wish to speak to Bentos."

The second guard pulled a writing slate from his satchel and took Michael's information. "Follow me."

The guard led him through the gates, through the courtyard and into the keep. A wide hallway led straight to an elaborate set of wooden doors. A sun was engraved on the left, and a moon was on the right. "Wait here." The guard knocked three times, then entered. Michael could see the dais through the open door. A halo of gold light surrounded Bentos, and a cooler white one around Delwyn. Was this what Halenka experienced seeing auras?

The guard spoke quietly to Bentos, then returned to gesture Michael inside before closing the door behind him.

Bentos had a fiery red mane of hair and a full beard and ruddy complexion. In contrast, Delwyn was pale with long black hair.

As Michael approached, it was clear that the two were continuing a frequent argument. Michael hesitated at the foot of the dais, afraid to interrupt.

"It is not safe for them here. We should move the children to the moon," Delwyn pleaded.

"You know as well as I that they can only age and grow down here on the earth. They would never reach their full potential."

"But they would be healthy and safe!"

"Let's give this young man a chance. If he fails as well... then we can revisit this conversation." He gently reached out a large hand to hold hers. "I love them, too. We also need to make sure this world is safe for your unborn child. The girls at least have had time to grow and learn. We don't want to curse a child to be forever a babe."

Delwyn pressed a hand to her belly. "You are right. Of course."

Bentos faced Michael. "My apologies. This has been a harrowing time. The girls complain of aches and fatigue. Their feet are red with sores. They spend their mornings soaking in the baths and having their feet tended. Their afternoons are time for their studies and personal projects. We have the finest tutors from all the land, and usually they soak up the knowledge eagerly. But they cannot stay awake during lessons and find no interest in their other activities."

Delwyn nodded. "We have tried watching them at night, but something blocks our vision from afar. And if one of us stays in person, we see nothing. So, either whatever is occurring happens only when we are not there, or it is simply something we cannot perceive. We cannot stay in their rooms every night."

"If you take up this task, you will stay in an adjoining room. We will give you three nights to solve this mystery. We simply cannot afford more time than that. The girls are too weak."

"You are our last hope, Michael. If you save our daughters, any boon you desire will be yours. Do you take upon yourself this task?"

This was it. His last chance to back out. Michael thought of his sisters, and of the muses. All girls deserved to live freely, deserved more than he could ever give them. "I do."

Bentos summoned a matronly woman with graying brown hair pulled into a practical bun. Her garb was simple and practical as well, a sturdy cotton dress with a long apron down the front.

"This is Daniella. She is the headmistress, in charge of the girls' learning and will know their whereabouts at this time of day. She will also get you settled in the guest room and handle anything else you might require."

Daniella curtsied to Bentos and turned to Michael. "So you're the next would-be-hero. What's your name?" He introduced himself. She looked him over with a scrutinizing gaze before nodding. "Come this way then."

Michael followed the headmistress through a maze of halls, into a conservatory. Light shined through the green tinted glass. Birds flitted through the trees, frogs croaked from a nearby fountain, and other creatures moved through the lush plants. The aroma of dirt and greenery was invigorating.

"This is Tesni's domain. Every time she steps outside, she returns with a new creature to care for. Normally, you could follow her voice as she sings to them. But she doesn't have the energy these days." They followed a stone path to the back, where a nest of pillows and blankets spread out in a select spot of sun. A girl, more of a woman not much younger than himself, stretched out in the midst, half covered by a half dozen sleeping cats.

"Tesni! Visitor!"

The girl sat up with a start. A cat yowled in protest as it fell off her shoulders. Tesni shook her red curls out of her face and looked up. Her eyes were nearly as red as her hair. She narrowed her eyes at Michael.

"Tesni, this is Michael. He will be observing you girls for the next few days."

"Another one? Can't they leave us alone? Just let us sleep." She flopped back down and pulled a pillow over her face.

"I apologize. Tesni may be the oldest, but they are all acting like spoiled children lately. I do hope you can figure out what's going on. For all our sakes. Hopefully Tesni will be more functional by dinner. To the next group, then."

Daniella gave a little background on the way. "The next three are actually triplets. Not that you could tell from their looks. They bicker with each other. More lately than usual." She led Michael into an art studio and introduced the three girls in their later teens.

Anwen, a tall blonde in a pink dressing gown, lazed back on a settee, arm dramatically thrown above her head.

Kala's dark brown hair was cut in a more practical bob. She sat in front of an easel, but gazed more through the canvas, paintbrush half forgotten in her fingers. A paint splattered smock covered a lilac silk pajama set.

The third was the most active of the sisters yet. Meinir danced with a mannequin wearing a ball gown, her own blue sundress floating about her as she spun. She was slender and tall, about Michael's own height, with long auburn curls.

Daniella sighed. "Meinir's dancing has improved at least. She could probably dance in her sleep without mis-stepping."

At that comment, Meinier stopped and peeked from behind the mannequin. "Sisters, Daniella brought a boy. Someone near our age, for once!"

Kala looked indifferent, but Anwen sat up and tidied her hair as she looked up at Michael. "I'm sure we'll be seeing much of each other over the next few days." She bit her lip and fluttered her eyelashes. She was certainly pretty, in a porcelain doll sort of way, but needed to work on her flirting.

"Now is not the time for that, Anwen." Daniella scolded. "Michael is here for business, not pleasure. You can flirt all you want when he's done here. Assuming he survives." Daniella mumbled the last part under her breath, but Michael was close enough to hear it. He waved both hello and goodbye to the girls as the headmistress whisked him off to the next room.

They found Gwynaeth in the courtyard, surrounded by the servants' children. She lay prone on a stone bench with her eyes closed, her golden hair in double braids that fell down either side to the ground. "Now go hide. I'll find you." She mumbled, "Eventually. After a nap." The children giggled and scattered out into the bushes and statuary.

"Gwyn here would normally run around with them. Again, no energy."

Gwynaeth waved a hand in acknowledgment, but said no more.

Enid was in the library. Though the youngest sister so far, probably mid teens, she had her earthy brown hair done up the same as Daniella. She had fallen asleep with a book on her lap.

"Enid is my best student. She always takes things seriously. Unlike her sisters. But even she can't get through one of my lessons these days. We sent the rest of the tutors home on extended holiday. Hard to keep them on when the girls can't sit through a class without falling asleep. Well, one more. Then I'll take you to your room."

Daniella had to stop and asked some of the other staff to find where Carys was. The girl was holding court in one of the guest rooms. A line of servants, mostly young women, trailed outside her door. They scurried out of the way at Daniella's approach. Carys looked to be around Saida's age, just blossoming into her teens. She sat across a table, holding the palms of a maid who was still just a teen herself. Her strawberry blonde hair fell in sheets as she leaned forward intently. Her eyes were puffy and red, but she seemed to have more energy than most of her sisters.

Carys nodded sagely. "Yes, I sense you will have success with Rodrick. Your energies align and he may just become the love of your life."

Daniella whispered to Michael, so as not to interrupt. "Rodrick is a stableboy. Carys here is our resident matchmaker. She even tried to set me up with one of the tutors!"

Michael grinned. "Was she wrong about your match?"

Daniella flushed. "I didn't have time to find out. He was only here a fortnight before he was sent away with the rest." After the maid left, a grin on her face, Daniella introduced Michael to Carys.

"And that's the last of them. I'll see you to your rooms to get settled, then call you later for dinner, where you will converse with all the girls. Thankfully, food seems to perk them up."

Daniella described the guest room as sparse, but it was a palace in itself to Michael. The four-poster bed was as big as his bedroom. He set his pack on a desk that sat below the window overlooking the sea. His one spare set of clothes seemed lonely in the spacious wardrobe. He hadn't bothered bringing nightclothes, as the mysterious happenings with the muses took place at night. Halenka said to meet her at sundown. He wondered where she was, hoping she had made it inside. In order to be prepared for whatever the night had in store, he opted to take a nap. Why let that gorgeous bed go to waste?

He woke to a knock on the door. The maid he'd seen with Carys earlier poked her head in. "Dinner is prepared. If you would follow me to the dining hall."

"Where is the headmistress?"

"Arousing the muses, ensuring they are all dressed proper for dinner."

The dining table was wide enough for both Bentos and Delwyn to sit side by side at the head. Carys and the triplets sat on one side of the table. The other muses sat on the other, leaving one chair for Michael next to Enid.

Enid, who had been sleeping with a book when Michael first saw her, leaned over and whispered to Gwynaeth. "Who is this?"

Gwyn rolled her eyes. "The new babysitter."

Anwen gave Michael a shy wave from across the table.

Michael introduced himself again for the benefit of those girls who were sleeping or inattentive during the initial introductions. He felt very flushed and out of place. He was sitting at a table with the gods and their daughters. How was this real? He felt very under-dressed in his simple brown tunic and trousers. At least they were clean and in good repair. Everyone else wore soft gowns and tunics with gold embroidery. Did he feel so warm because Bentos radiated heat? Or was it just the circumstance?

Delwyn thanked Michael for joining them and implored him to ask anything he had need of.

Michael drooled over the plate of food that was set before him. Pork and vegetables and sweet breads. Nothing he wouldn't eat at home, just more elevated. So much flavor and moisture. Guilt tainted it for a moment, that his sisters were having leftover stew while he feasted. He reminded himself that he was doing this for them. If he could solve this problem for the gods, they would grant a boon, something he could use to give his sisters a better life.

Remembering his purpose fueled his confidence. Halenka had said the muses went to the Gloaming Realm at night. He wondered if they would admit to it. "Forgive my boldness, but what do you girls get up to at night?"

Tesni, as the eldest, took the lead. Her answer sounded quite rote. "We retire to bed. We wake in the morning exhausted as if we had a restless night but can recall none of it. Only feel our aches and pains and fatigue."

Michael watched the girls as she answered, but none looked suspicious. Either they truly didn't remember what happened, or they were very good at hiding it.

Delwyn added, "The girls have their own suites, but we began grouping them all into one room to keep a better eye on them. Though even locking their door at night has changed nothing. Your room opens to theirs, so you may observe them. I do hope you have better success than your predecessors."

"And we trust you will be fully respectful of the girls. You wouldn't survive if we suspected anything untoward," Bentos warned.

"I will give your daughters all the same respect I do to my own sisters."

After dinner, everyone retired to their rooms. Michael noted the sun was going down. Hopefully, he could sneak out and meet

Halenka soon. He noted the direction the servers left so he could find the kitchen.

A crackling fire welcomed him in his bedroom. Michael waited in his room for an hour, hoping that would give enough time for Halenka to get in place and the kitchens to clear out. To calm his mind, he set up his incense burner. He scattered his Confidence blend in the lit ashes. The blend of frankincense and cinnamon was woodsy with notes of citrus.

He could hear the muses talking on the other side of the door adjoining the two bedrooms. He couldn't make out the words, but the sounds calmed him. Reminded him of being at home with his own sisters.

Once his incense burned out, Michael lit a candle. As he reached for the door, a knock came from the other side. He opened it to find a servant with his head bowed and hands up, offering a glass of wine. "A nightcap for you, sir. To calm your nerves."

"Thank you," Michael said. He took the glass and closed the door.

The wine was deep red, with sparkles of gold. It smelled earthy and sweet. He was suddenly quite thirsty and tempted, but something held him back. Perhaps it was the lingering smell of the incense's contrasting aroma, or the sharp memory of Halenka's story of fae wine. If there was any chance this was the same thing, he'd be safer avoiding it. He set the glass on the desk. He poked his head out the door to make sure the servant was gone, then headed toward where the kitchen should be.

Michael followed Halenka's notion and let his nose lead him. It was a straight enough path to the kitchens. The kitchen was as large as the dining hall. And it smelled glorious. He wanted to poke his head in all the jars of spices and peek into the pots. But he focused and crossed the room to the door to the yard. He didn't see anyone outside, just empty gardens. Something poked him in the side, causing him to yelp.

"It's me," Halenka said. She lowered her hood, seeming to appear from nowhere.

"That thing really works. Follow me; I don't want to leave the muses unattended for too long."

Halenka pulled her hood back up, and they returned to his room.

Michael leaned his ear to the adjoining door and heard soft laughter from the other room. They should still have a bit of time.

Halenka gasped, and Michael turned to see what was wrong. She held the goblet of wine, all color drained from her face.

"It's fae wine, isn't it?"

She nodded.

"It smells amazing. What is the wine made from?"

Halenka looked nauseous. Her voice was tight. "Ambrosia fruits, mixed with the blood of a fae, and sprinkled with pixie dust. That's... what happened to my sister. Killed for a few bottles of wine. Between the wine and the other drugs the Underking is making, the pixies are nearing extinction, as the dust comes from their crushed wings. Pixie dust is quite addictive."

Michael paled as well. He was more than grateful he had resisted drinking that wine. "The mystery of the muses has been going on for three months. If the muses have been drinking it as well, then that means..."

Halenka nodded soberly. "I don't know how many bottles each batch makes, but too many fae and pixie sacrificed for each."

"No wonder you fled. That's madness. All the more reason for this to stop. It's hurting your people and mine." He reached out to take her hands in his. "I vow to stop this. To honor your sister and prevent more innocent deaths."

A sad smile graced her lips. "Thank you, Michael. You are truly an honorable man."

The other room had quieted. Perhaps too much. Had the girls fallen asleep? Time to do his duty. Michael opened the door, hoping all the girls were decent. The room, which would have been spacious, had three beds squeezed in. The triplets lay together on one, limbs entangled. Two sisters shared each of the other beds.

"There," Halenka said. She pointed to a dresser on the far side of the room. A bottle of wine and seven glasses lined the top. Michael rushed over. The bottle was empty. It smelled the same as the glass he had been given.

"What does the wine do exactly—" a groaning of hinges interrupted him. The room went dark as the fire in the fireplace vanished. Then the air filled with dancing lights, just like those Halenka had conjured before. The muses were no longer sleeping in their beds; they stood together in the center of the room.

Meinir chided her sisters. "Hurry, hurry! Get out of these sad nightgowns."

Michael paled, imagining them disrobing in front of him. Bentos would burn him alive. But he needn't have worried. Each girl waved her hands and magically changed their simple nightgowns into dresses worthy of the grandest ball. Each wore their signature color in dress, slippers, and mask. He expected them to be bedecked in jewelry as well, but the only item he saw was a moonstone ring glinting on Tesni's right hand.

Meinir noticed Michael and Halenka, who had been too startled to resume her hidden nature. "Who are you? No matter. Your clothes simply won't do. You can't go to a masquerade like that!

Why do none of our guests come well dressed?" She put a hand on his shoulder, and then Halenka. Their clothes transformed. Michael now wore an elegant black suit, perfectly tailored to him. Halenka wore a diaphanous gown in the palest of blue, the color of her eyes. She still wore a cloak, but it had transformed as well, into a soft velvety blue gray, lined with a darker blue. She looked like a fae queen.

Kala held out a mask for her to complete the look. The mask was silver butterfly wings edged in blue. She handed Michael a black simple eye mask. He was fine with its more subdued simplicity. No one would look at him next to all these beauties.

Another rumble, and the stone in the back of the fireplace disappeared, opening to a glittering tunnel, lit by more of the floating lights.

A cohort of people dressed as swans swooped in. They wore white feather masks with beaks, and feather capes attached to their arms. They rushed in to surround the girls and escort them through the mysterious tunnel. Halenka pulled up her hood before she was noticed. Michael's fear of being left behind was quickly dispelled as two swans flew in, enveloping him with their arm wings and leading him into the tunnel. Michael could feel Halenka's hand firmly holding onto his as they were swept along.

The tunnel traveled at a leisurely downward rate, in a subtle curve. If Michael oriented them correctly, he believed they were going toward the sea. Eventually, the tunnel opened into a wide cavern. It was like no cave Michael had ever seen. There were trees, but not normal trees. The branches and leaves glinted like silver. Michael reached out and broke a small twig off of one as they went by. After a time, they entered a new grove of trees, this one of gold. Then a third of diamonds, glittering in the fairy lights. He took a branch from each. Perhaps it would be proof enough to Bentos of where the muses went at night.

Then, like in Halenka's fae tale, they heard joyous laughter ahead. The trees ahead wove together into latticework, creating a large domed hall. Here, all three types of trees wove together—silver, gold, and diamond, with golden fruit dangling from the branches. Michael grabbed one of those as well. It was about the size of an apricot, but with smooth golden skin like an apple. He pierced the skin, and it broke easily, letting out sweet smelling juices. He licked his finger. Sweet like honey, and just that taste caused a terrible thirst for more. This must be that ambrosia fruit.

"What are you doing?" Halenka hissed at him. She snatched the fruit from his hand and threw it to the ground. "Did you eat any of it? How stupid are you?"

"I didn't eat any." But oh, did he want to. "I'll be fine."

There wasn't one large fire, but a dozen braziers encircling the space. Countless people danced in and out of the light. It was hard to focus here. He concentrated on the feel of Halenka's hand in his, let it anchor him.

Partners approached the muses, and they began to dance with the rest. And dance and dance. It was dizzying. He took Halenka in his arms and joined the dancers. He looked into her brilliant eyes, no longer thinking of the muses, only the beautiful girl he held in his arms. Maybe it was something in the air, or the taste of ambrosia, but that was the last thing he remembered, and he lost the rest of the night.

He woke up in the enormous bed, with the morning light streaming through the window, and Halenka glowering down at him. His head pounded and his feet hurt. Was this how the muses felt each morning? "What happened last night?"

"You tasted the ambrosia fruit. You danced off and ignored me and your duty to watch the muses. What do you remember?"

"I remember our clothes transforming." Which was apparently permanent, as he still wore the suit. "Following the swans and muses down the tunnel, through the groves, and into the dancing hall. Not much after that." He checked his pockets and pulled out the contents. He still had the three sprigs of silver, gold, and diamond.

"But what of the rest of the night? What happens to the muses? Did you see?"

"I was too busy following you and making sure you didn't eat or drink anything more. I didn't want you trapped there forever."

That was fair enough. He certainly hadn't expected that fruit to be so potent. The Gloaming Realm was a dangerous place.

Halenka sighed and sat next to him on the bed. "On the plus side, your dancing did blend in. I don't think you'll be able to get so close to the muses to find out what happens without more work."

"If only I could be as invisible as you."

A thoughtful look came over her face. "I may be able to extend my ability to you if you are similarly cloaked and smell more like a fae. Though you will have to stay in contact with me the whole time."

That was one thing Michael strongly remembered from the night before. Her soft hand in his. "I can do that."

Michael changed into his spare clothes, and Halenka stayed in the bedroom while he went to breakfast. Bentos and Delwyn were already well into their meal. The muses were not in attendance, so perhaps they were still sleeping.

Bentos greeted Michael. "I am glad you have joined us this morning. I was not sure we would see you again. Do you have anything to report?"

Michael presented his evidence so far: the sprigs of silver, gold, and diamond. "The muses are being led into the Gloaming Realm each night. They are drugged, which explains why they don't remember the next morning."

Storm clouds came over Bentos' face. "That explains why we couldn't view them. Our vision doesn't cross into the Gloaming Realm. We have no power there. What is being done to my daughters?"

Michael flushed. "That I do not know yet. I will gain more information tonight. But in order to do so, I have a request. I need a cloak. And I will need to return to my home for some things, but will be back before nightfall."

Delwyn provided him with a cloak pulled from the night sky. It was midnight blue, and he swore he saw stars when he looked long enough into its depths. It also had two generous inner pockets.

His sisters were out on their daily chores when Michael and Halenka returned to the house. In his workshop, he pulled out the branches again, and some basic ingredients. Michael scraped the bark off the branches into slivers. Each had a distinct scent. The aroma of the silver branch resembled the morning mists that wafted off the Sea of Mystery—damp, earthy, and slightly tinged with ozone. The gold branch smelled sweet but also had a woodsy aroma, reminiscent of honey-dipped pinecones. The sparkling diamond branch was effervescent, emitting a fruity floral scent like wild jasmine, sharpened by the smell of lightning. Michael combined the bark scrapings with different aromatics until he found one that Halenka approved of, enhancing the mossy wood aroma while leaving the subtle hints of sweetness.

Michael heated a large brazier and put in the new blend of incense, which he named Fae Night. Then he draped his new cloak to absorb the smoke. He hoped this would allow him to smell enough like a fae that Halenka could extend her magic to him. While they waited, they found some lunch and caught up with his sisters.

When they returned to the keep, Michael left the smoked cloak with Halenka. He changed into his fancy clothes from the night before. He'd feel much less under-dressed at dinner this time. The muses still remembered nothing from their nightly adventures. Michael snagged some rolls and a meat hand pie to take back to the room for Halenka. He was so grateful she was helping him with this. If not for her, he would probably still be dancing in the Gloaming Realm.

Halenka still wore the muse-created dress, as she didn't have a change of clothes. Each put on their masks. Halenka hid herself until a servant delivered a glass of wine again. Michael tried to get a good look at him, to see if he was a fae, but his eyes slid right off him, unable to focus.

They didn't waste any time dumping the glass into the fire, then barging in on the muses next door. They were just pouring their own glasses from a fresh bottle. Michael dashed over and knocked the bottle out of Anwen's hand. But Meinir gracefully snatched it out of the air. She nearly hissed at him, "How dare you! This is a gift for the muses! Who are you to interfere?" Enid growled and grabbed Michael's arm. He grew lightheaded, felt his life slipping away.

Halenka pulled Michael out of Enid's grasp. "It's too late. They are addicted to it. Their deity blood keeps them from falling fully under the spell, but they crave its taste."

The girls pounced on the wine, nearly ravenous. The wine took effect, and they drooped, falling to their beds. While Michael and Halenka waited for the next phase, they pulled their hoods up. Halenka grabbed Michael's hand and whispered calming words to him. The world seemed to dim for a moment as her magic settled around them.

When the fire disappeared into fairy lights, the muses awoke and were soon laughing and changing into their gowns. If they remembered the fight with Michael, they did not show it. They didn't seem to notice him at all, so he hoped Halenka's magic was working.

The night began the same as the one before, with fairy lights and swans to guide them through the glittering groves. This time, however, the swans ignored Michael. He rushed after the group, tightly gripping Halenka's hand, being careful not to make contact with any trees or fruit.

His thoughts remained focused, and he caught details he had previously overlooked. A group of humans danced blissfully together off to the side, occasionally drinking from glasses filled by unseen servants, or grabbing a fruit from a dangling vine.

Four imposing figures seemed to appear from nowhere, but their presence filled the space. The woman wore an octopus mask, tentacles looking nearly alive in the light as they hovered around her head. A young man wore a fox mask. Another, of indeterminate gender, wore a mask made of a deer skull, eyes hollow and haunting. There was no doubt that the fourth figure was the Underking, wearing a golden stag mask and an impressive crown of antlers. These must be the four siblings that Halenka had told him of. They murmured to each other before quietly departing to select separate muses as dance partners.

The deer drew Enid close. The woman danced with Kala. The fox approached Anwen. The Underking stole away with Tesni.

Michael and Halenka cautiously advanced, relying on the magic to conceal them from the four. He had to find out what they were saying and doing to those girls. They approached close enough to hear the Underking speaking quietly to Tesni.

The Underking ran a finger through Tesni's red curls. "Be my bride, my beautiful Tesni. Together, we can rule all the realms."

She hesitated but shook her head. "No, I cannot marry you." Despite her rebuttal, she still took his offered hand and joined the dance with him.

Enid and the deer engaged in a hushed discussion about the significance of life and death.

They shifted to the woman, but there was no talking. The woman's lips were locked with Kala's.

The fox didn't stay long with one girl, but bounced between the rest, saying things to make them laugh.

After a time, the muses began to slow and stumble. Their partners released them, the muses wandering off to get refreshment, while the four stepped off to the side. Michael and Halenka hurried over to hear their discussion.

"She is weakening," the Underking said. "A few more nights and she will be mine. Then we can do with the rest as we please."

"I wonder what wine of muse would taste like," said the deer.

Michael shuddered at the thought, and Halenka's nails dug into his hand.

The Underking laughed. "A fun thought, but we may need their power to overcome Bentos."

The woman purred, "Then the Realm of Dust will be ours. I look forward to finding some new playthings." She trailed a finger over her lips. "Though I have quite enjoyed the pleasure of these muses."

They intended to dethrone Bentos! And almost had the muses under their control. There wasn't much time to stop this.

Halenka looked as worried as Michael felt. They had to tell Bentos. He wanted to leave immediately, get out and warn him, but Michael spun around and no longer saw an exit. The branches and vines were a complete dome around them. They couldn't leave until the fae were ready.

His chest grew tight, and he struggled to breathe. "We can't leave. What do we do?"

Halenka turned him to face her and put her free hand on his cheek. "We wait. My magic is hiding us, but only so long as you are calm. Just relax. And dance with me."

Michael put his arms around Halenka and looked into her steady eyes. His breathing calmed as he focused on her touch, her smell. They danced until the branches opened and the swans came to nearly carry the exhausted muses back to their room.

Bentos boiled with the news of the Underking's schemes. Delwyn became a shadow of herself. They wanted to remove their daughters from danger immediately. Not give it another night.

Michael explained how the girls had acted with the wine. "I fear pulling them out without breaking their bond to the Gloaming would do more harm than good. You've seen how faded they have become. Each day, they sleep longer. Will they recover?"

Bentos clenched his fists on the table. "And what do you intend to do?"

"Break the enchantment. Give me this one more night, as you promised."

"Very well. Our fate lies in your hands."

They returned to the Kether cottage again. Their last experiment with the incense had been successful. Maybe they could make a new blend. Michael retrieved ingredients for an awakening ritual: lemon, white sage, althea, sandalwood, and honeysuckle. Clarity, vigor, true sight. He mixed it with the remaining branch shavings from the Gloaming Realm. He burned a small amount and breathed it in.

His mind opened, his vision sharpened. All the fatigue from the little sleep the last few nights vanished. As he turned to inquire about its impact on Halenka, a side effect of the incense distracted him. Halenka glowed. He could see her aura. A deep indigo.

"What is an indigo aura indicative of?"

"Someone in tune with their self, and of others. True empaths. Why do you ask?"

"I see your aura."

"We can never see our own aura. Indigo. Perhaps that is why I have the gift to see those of others. Is this because of the incense?"

"I think so." Michael opened the door and called out, "Daphne! Come to my workshop!"

After a moment, Daphne poked her head out from the girls' bedroom. "Your forbidden workshop? Are you sure?"

"Yes. Get in here."

Daphne scampered in, and Michael closed the door.

"Breathe in the smoke."

"Ooh, a new incense?" She leaned in and coughed. "That smells strange. What is in it?" She turned and gasped. "I can see your colors! Does that mean I'm a fae, too?"

Halenka cupped the girl's face. "As delightful as that would be for me, I'm afraid not. It's just the magic of the incense. It won't last."

"I'm glad I can see like you, even if it's just for a bit. Oh!" She bounced on her toes. "I can go see what my sisters' colors are!" And off she dashed again, somehow even more energetic than when she arrived.

Michael shrugged. "Well, there's no promise it will wake the muses, but it is potent. It's worth a try."

"And you will see more. Things I have witnessed but cannot speak of."

Michael smoked his midnight cloak again in Fae Night to freshen the scent, then filled its pockets with packets of the Awakening mixture. This time they didn't interfere with the muses as they drank their wine and changed, merely waited and followed.

His senses still tingled from breathing in the new mix himself. The muses' auras closely matched their signature colors. Their auras weren't as bright as Halenka's.

The Old Ones were dressed and masked the same, except for the fox, who tonight looked distinctly female instead of the young man of the night before, in an elaborate red dress that rivaled those of the muses. The four had harsh auras, deep hues tainted by an oily darkness. Once they took their muse partners, Michael could see what Halenka had alluded to. The powerful fae were siphoning off the muses' auras, their life-force, draining the girls and strengthening their own power.

"This is what you saw but couldn't speak of. What the Under-king is truly doing to the muses."

Halenka nodded, but did not speak. Her king still had power over her.

With the Old Ones focused, it was time for action. Michael handed half of the pouches to Halenka. "We split up, make this as quick as possible. Drop one of these in each of the braziers. Awaken the entire space."

Halenka tightened her grip on his hand. "But won't you become visible once we separate? I don't know how to keep the hidden magic going if we are not linked."

"I'm willing to take that chance."

She surprised him with a firm kiss on his lips. "Be safe."

He wanted to linger, to taste her mouth, but she was off.

No one looked his way as he wove between dancers to the edge of the room. The cloak, made of magic, had absorbed enough of the hidden fae magic that it had become truly enchanted.

The first few pouches were slow to smoke and made little impact. By the last one, Michael was hearing less laughter and more horror. It was working. He saw the group of humans looking around with fresh eyes. The muses were pulling away from their partners, their auras still weak, but no longer draining away. The Underking still had a grip on Tesni. Michael hurried over to help her.

Tesni was screaming at him. "I will never be yours! You are a monster!"

"You want to see a monster?" The Underking's fingers extended into sharp claws. He pulled back his hand to lash out. Michael barreled between them, breaking the Underking's hold on Tesni and knocking her back. But the attack still followed through, claws tearing into Michael's cheek. He stumbled back. "Halenka, get them out of here!"

The seven awakened muses, along with the group of previously enchanted humans, fought back against the fae, whose powers seemed to be muted by the same smoke that heightened the others. The muses joined hands, their combined power making the earth tremble. Fruit and leaves fell from the shaking branches. Halenka rushed to Michael's side. "They can handle themselves now. Let's get you out of here."

The latticework of branches wilted and died, revealing the path out through the grove. Michael waved the other humans forward ahead of them. He glanced back to see where the Old Ones were, but they had already disappeared. Halenka pulled him, and they returned to the keep with the others. Over a dozen people crowded the muses' bedroom.

"Where are the muses?" Michael almost went back. Just as the stone of the fireplace began to close, the muses came through.

Despite their wild hair filled with twigs and leaves, the sisters appeared more alert and energetic than Michael had ever witnessed. Their eyes glowed with righteous fury.

Tesni came to Michael and lowered herself into a deep curtsy. "On behalf of my sisters, I thank you for saving us."

Echoes of thanks came from the others in the room. Michael recognized a few now. The missing petitioners who had come to solve the mystery of the muses. So many trapped by the fae.

The door burst open and Delwyn rushed in. "I felt the surge of magic. My daughters, you are glowing again. You're back. For good now?"

Gwynaeth was the first to embrace her mother. "Yes, we are free. All will be well. Where's father?"

"He is containing himself in our chambers, so his emotions do not scorch the earth. Go to him, reassure him."

Gwyn rushed out, followed closely by most of her sisters.

Tesni hesitated, looking down at her bare hands. "Mother, my ring. It's gone. I must have lost it down there. What if... what if *he* has it?"

Delwyn took her daughter's hands. "Then we will hope he doesn't realize its power. But we dare not send anyone back to retrieve it. Your safety is more important."

Tesni frowned but nodded and left to join her sisters.

The Moon Goddess looked around at those who remained. "All of you. We thought you were lost. Thank you for risking your lives for our daughters. I am sorry for your loss of time. You will be compensated." She turned to Michael and smiled. "And you. You did what they could not. But you are injured." She gestured him forward and put her hand on his torn cheek. "I can stop the bleeding, but the wounds are deep. Who did this to you?"

"The Underking."

"Mahallaliel. His power is too strong. It will heal, but there will be a scar. Rest up for now. Meet us in the throne room at midday. You shall have the greatest boon."

Michael and Halenka retreated to the adjoining room and collapsed together on the bed.

Halenka propped herself up on an elbow and gazed down at him. "You did it. I knew you could."

He lifted a hand and traced from the tip of her ear, down to her chin. "I couldn't have done any of this without you." Talking still hurt a bit, and he brought his hand back to cover his wounds. "Definitely didn't come out unscathed."

"You should not hide your wounds. They are a mark of your bravery." She kissed him again. This time, Michael held on, deepening the kiss. She tasted as sweet as the ambrosia, and just as addictive. He pulled back and looked into her eyes. "Stay with me."

"Always."

Michael insisted Halenka accompany him to his audience with the sky gods. She seemed nervous, but stayed with him as promised.

Bentos and Delwyn sat on their thrones. Their seven daughters stood off to the side, hands held, united. Michael could no longer see their auras, but they looked stronger still.

Bentos smiled down at Michael. "Thank you for freeing my daughters. We will take measures against the fae to stop their plotting." His expression darkened, the fiery aura surrounding him pulsing with dangerous heat. "Though I see you brought a fae with you."

Michael felt Halenka pull back, wishing she could disappear again. He took her hand in his. "This is Halenka. She helped me every step of the way. I would not have survived these last three nights without her."

"Is that true?"

Halenka nodded shyly.

"Did you know of my cousin's plans?"

"I... I cannot say."

Bentos studied her intently. "I see. You are under a geas. Bonded to him, as likely all his subjects are. He is not a benevolent ruler." Delwyn placed a hand on her husband's knee. He placed a hand on hers, breathed deeply, and his aura calmed. "I promised a boon for those who helped my daughters. Would you like me to break your geas?"

Halenka's head whipped up, hope in her eyes. "You can free me from him?"

The Sun King nodded. "If that is your desire."

"Yes. Yes, thank you."

Bentos put out his hand and a nearly blinding flash of light surrounded Halenka. She stumbled to her knees and sobbed.

Michael helped her up. "Are you well?"

She looked up at him with tears in her eyes. "Yes. I have never felt freer. I could see so many terrible things my king did, but I could not act or speak against him. Not directly."

"Now it is your turn, Michael," Bentos said. "We promised a boon. What is it you desire?"

"I only want for my sisters to be cared for. Food on the table, a warm home. Perhaps money for any schooling they may desire."

Bentos opened his mouth to respond, but Delwyn interrupted.

"Don't grant that," she said. "Michael, you deserve so much more. You are noble, hardworking, willing to sacrifice yourself and your desires for those around you. You had great wisdom and clarity in saving our daughters. Even saw the value of help from an unlikely source in Halenka here. We cannot continue to remain among you. I believe you are the perfect man to reign in our place. The keep, the riches, the land—all of it will be yours."

Epilogue

B entos' voice boomed across the land. "Pay respects to Michael of Kether, the new King of Tessagonia. Honor him as I do."

The Sky Gods made a deal with the Old Ones, that no gods would remain in the Realm of Dust. If any returned, there would be war. Man may be influenced, but not ruled.

And thus the fae, and the creatures of the night and of the deeps, were banished to separate realms. The Old Ones were separated so that they could no longer scheme and combine their powers. Mahallaliel, the Underking, sentenced to be trapped in his Gloaming Realm below. Kabarac, the Trickster, to be forever wandering in the shadows and only able to reveal himself in the darkest of nights, the new moon. Shamanuc, the Whisperer, banished beyond the mirror, trapped between the realms of life and death. And Velekai, the Drowned, to never touch her sea home and remain in the waters of the open ocean. The sky gods had a lesser hold over the Outer Isles and the waters beyond. Thus, these ancient, ravenous gods claimed authority over them, yearning to regain their power.

Bentos and Delwyn made a new home in the sky, creating a new kingdom, Lesenti, above the Sea of Mystery, where the muses could safely observe the land of Tessagonia and visit as they pleased. To protect their newborn child, they took him across the ocean, out of reach of the Old Ones.

Michael of Kether married Halenka the Fae, and they became the new rulers of Tessagonia in Bentos' absence. They helped to watch over the muses, raising them alongside Michael's own sisters, until they each became of age and permanently made their home in Lesenti. Rumors are that a passage still exists between the castle and the clouds.

In thanks, the muses returned at the birth of the new royal child to give their blessings.

To this day, the Kether lineage still carries fae blood, and a child each generation is born with magical gifts.

Author's Note

The Gloaming Realm was based on the Twelve Dancing Princesses. I may not have twelve, but I do have seven muse sisters. The plan to have this end in exile of the old ones was there from the beginning, but I initially was going to have the Underking luring the seven muses for his own sons. Instead, I focused on his own greed for power.

The name Michael comes from Andrew Lang's version of the story. He was also a peasant in that tale, but here I gave him some skills that would be useful in solving the mystery. Halenka comes from a variant called The Three Girls. In that story, Halenka was a fairy who aided the hero.

Other elements I kept were the drugged wine (with my variation of course), the groves of silver, gold, and diamond (inspiration for the leaves on my ebook cover), and the disappearance of previous people who attempted to solve the mystery. The swan costumes for the fae that escort the muses down to the Gloaming Realm is a nod to the swan boats that carry the princesses. And of course the invisibility cloak!

The typical reward for this tale is marriage to one of the princesses. That wouldn't work for my immortal muses, but I did find a way for Michael to be rewarded with a crown.

The ending of this story both explains some of the traditions (the muses bearing gifts to newborn royalty), gives more back-ground into the old ones, and sets up for future tales (the muses have a brother, a missing ring, fae blood in the Kether line, a passage to the realm of the muses). The rough draft also alluded to a future civil war, but I figured that was getting into too many elements. War still happens, it just isn't foreshadowed here.

Easter Egg: A note about Daphne. Daphne/Daphnia is a name you'll see come up in many of my stories. She represents my inner child. Usually a young girl with blonde hair in pigtails. Curious and optimistic. Something you can look for in my future novels.

The Moon Prince

Mary W. Jensen

Contents

1

Tessagonia is not the only land in this world. To the north is a land of ever-winter. To the east is a paradise, free of Man, where mythical creatures dwell. Across the sea to the west lies the land of Kenaleko. A wide river splits this round continent in two, with the center diverting to encircle the towering Mount Ojai. Occupying the eastern half of the continent is the prosperous and fertile kingdom of Moshotan.

In the mountain's shadow lived Keizo Suto, a simple bamboo cutter, and his wife Rika. Married for many years, they could not have children of their own. Each day, Keizo would go out into the bamboo grove to cut down canes he could use to make furniture for their humble cottage, and to sell what he could to provide for them.

One day, Keizo found something unusual in the grove—a soft glow coming from the bamboo canes ahead. The light was coming from a large bamboo shoot. The bamboo cutter dug up the shoot and peeled off the tough outer leaves. To his surprise, instead of the usual tender meat, he revealed a baby. The baby itself glowed, like the moon above. He knew this was the answer to his wife's prayers. A child to call their own.

Rika was surprised at her husband's early return home, and even more surprised at the bundle he revealed. With its strange arrival, they knew this was no mere lost or abandoned child. It was their duty now to raise him. They named the boy Akihiko, their Bright Prince.

They hired a nursemaid from the village to feed the infant. The bamboo cutter had little to pay her, but promised to do what he could. As the nursemaid had three children of her own, one just weaned, she merely wanted to help the child.

Keizo made a bamboo cradle, then returned to work in the grove. But the wonders did not stop there. That day, a stalk of bamboo glowed. He cut it open, and in the hollow stem was a gold coin. Joyously, he returned home to pay the nursemaid. Each day, a new stalk glowed, providing him with a gold coin or a gem.

With this new wealth, they could easily provide for their son. They built a grander home and hired servants, enabling the couple to spend more time with Akihiko. They hired tutors for the boy, to give him the best education. The hired staff helped with the household, but Keizo alone went to the grove each morning. Others had looked to see where the wealth came from, but the stalks glowed for him alone. In time, they extended their land, with additional buildings and a meditation garden, and a high outer wall for privacy.

The boy also continued to glow. He was a calm child, and that calmness radiated to those around him. As Akihiko grew older, he realized he was not like other children. He questioned his parents. "Why am I different from everyone? I glow at night, and since the new tutor has taught me meditation, I am having visions. He said that's not normal. Is something wrong with me?"

Keizo asked, "What do you see in these visions?"

"Other lands and strange people and beasts. Sometimes I know things, and I don't know how."

"You are different. Special. Your mother and I were never able to have children. I found you in the bamboo grove, a gift from the gods. But though you are not of our loins, you are the child of our heart and will always be our son."

Akihiko became determined to learn more about this world he caught glimpses of. He sought books to fill his room, losing himself in both history and poetry. Despite the servants and the wealth, he insisted on learning to do tasks with his own hands—cooking, cleaning, tapestry, music. As Aki grew in stature, he grew in beauty. His black hair grew long, his face wise. By age twenty, word had spread of this glowing beauty.

2

People of all ages and genders came to glimpse the man they were calling the Moon Prince. Akihiko did not like all the attention. He couldn't understand why he was getting so much interest. He requested that the estate's gates remain shut, with no visitors, and spent most of his time indoors.

Over time, most of the spectators gave up and returned to their homes. Five remained, determined to not only see this Moon Prince, but to court him. They played musical instruments in the hopes he would hear. Sent gifts of food and fine cloth. Occasionally, they would catch a glimpse as Akihiko listened at a window or meditated in the garden. This only encouraged them further. United in their cause, they would help each other, boost one up to look over the walls, or give feedback on a poem or song.

The determination of these suitors impressed Keizo and Rika. After weeks of their dedication, Keizo and Rika approached their son. "Akihiko, I am old, over seventy years in age. And your mother isn't getting any younger either. You should marry. Make an old man happy in his retirement."

Akihiko sat in his room, the suitors' gifts surrounding him. He lifted the edge of a tapestry. "I don't understand all this. These people don't even know me. What if I'm not as beautiful as they think? Or worse, what if my appearance is all they see, and they don't know my heart?"

Rika knelt by Akihiko and took his hands in her own. "So, give them a chance. Meet these suitors, allow them to see you. They will see what I do, a calm, kind natured man with a beautiful heart. If nothing else, it will be good for you to interact with new people. You may have much knowledge from your books and your visions, but you have been sheltered here."

Aki sighed. "Very well. I will meet with them at least."

He still refused to let them inside his home but agreed to meetings in the meditation garden. Here Akihiko was most comfortable, surrounded by bamboo stalks, the splashing of the koi pond, the birds in the air. He sat on his meditation rock, much worn from these past years. Finding solace in his peaceful moment, he decided to put these suitors to the test. He would meet with them one at a time and give each a task to complete by his next birthday.

The first suitor was Seru, a young woman from a noble house. Her jet-black hair rivaled Aki's in length. She wore an elaborate embroidered robe. She bowed gracefully "Moon Prince, it is a pleasure to be in your presence."

"Akihiko. I am no prince."

"You are certainly no mere man. Marry me and we will be lord and lady over my family's lands."

"It is too soon to talk of marriage. Before I could even consider it, I require of you a task. Bring me an object of my desire."

Seru had wealth to spare. She felt she could afford any gift he sought. "Name your price."

"There is a place in the Gloaming Realm where trees of silver, gold, and diamond have woven together to be one. Bring me one of these branches, and the golden fruit that grows from it. Present it to me on my twenty-first birthday in seven months' time."

Seru returned to her friends to discuss this strange request. The Gloaming Realm was a place of stories. Who knew if such a tree even existed? But precious metals and gems were something that could be bought. Seru travelled to the great cities and asked for the most talented jewelers, only speaking with those skilled in the right materials. Family funds covered the purchase of raw gold and silver, and the best quality diamonds. She hired a blacksmith to work hand in hand with the six of the most talented jewelers she could find, promising them fame and wealth at the end of their task. She hid them all away in a remote cabin, explaining her need. They began to plan how to make such a branch.

Regularly, Seru would check in on their progress, dismissing their creations and providing feedback. Too thick, too small, too fragile, or clearly different parts, or the golden fruit was an odd shape. She demanded the best of their craftsmanship. With a month to the Moon Prince's birthday, Seru was finally satisfied with their creation—a delicate branch woven of distinct gold and silver, and inlaid with diamonds, with matching leaves, and a small gold fruit attached to the end.

Shotaro came from a noble family as well, but was the youngest child with three elder brothers. This gave him the freedom to choose a spouse of his own liking without having to worry about producing an heir. He glossed his long black hair to vie with the natural shine of Seru's.

Shotaro was taller than Akihiko, and felt awkward standing while the other sat. Sitting on the ground would prove more uncomfortable, however. He waved down the servant who had escorted him in, requesting a stool to sit upon.

Akihiko shifted impatiently, but Shotaro waited until he had properly seated himself to address his host.

"My lord Akihiko, you do me great honor to meet with me today."

"I am no lord, merely a man."

"Perhaps no lord, but you have wealth and greatness! You are the talk of the kingdom."

Akihiko sighed. "I ask of you a task, as I do the others. Bring me the pearl heart of a sea dragon." Shotaro paled at the explanation of what was required, but assured Akihiko he was up to the task.

Sea dragons were merely one of the dangers of the oceans separating continents. Shotaro hadn't even known they had pearl hearts. He did happen to have a cousin who captained a whaling vessel.

His cousin thought him crazy, first for wanting to marry a man he had only met once, and second for wanting to hunt a sea dragon. "You do not know how my job even works. We don't have just one ship, but many, to encircle the whale and drive it to shallow water."

"But you have harpoons!" Shotaro protested. "Can't we just hunt one out at sea? Or drive it to shore like you do the whales?"

"Whales are large and docile; a sea dragon would tear my wide wooden ship asunder. If you see the glow in the water that signifies a sea dragon, you turn ship and leave the area. It is not worth it!"

Shotaro insisted, so off he and his cousin went into the ocean with the entire whaling fleet. The fleet would focus on its normal whaling, and if the head ship happened to come across a dragon, they would try their techniques on it. However, Shotaro would be accountable for compensating any lost personnel or vessels. If he could be the one to claim Akihiko's heart (and treasury), it would be worth whatever price his cousin demanded.

Shotaro, however, did not have the sea legs, or the stomach, of his cousin. A week into the journey, he was miserable, barely able to stand, and unable to keep food down. His cousin dropped him off back at Moshotan, having never even sighted a sea dragon. Shotaro tried to convince him to continue the hunt without him, but his cousin was done with the entire matter.

Other fishers and captains he talked to laughed him off. Giving up on ever acquiring a real dragon pearl, Shotaro acquired the next best thing. He hired a potter to make one out of clay. He had to spend plenty of time in dingy seaside taverns listening to tales of dragons to get a proper description of the size and color of a dragon's heart. By the time the task was done, he loathed even the smell of the sea and returned with the false pearl to his family home, well inland, to wait until Akihiko's birthday.

Endo wasn't considered one of the pretty suitors. He was short, balding, and wore spectacles. He didn't come from nobility or have wealth of his own. A simple farmer, older than the others, he hadn't found a soul mate, and felt he deserved love too. He was as smitten with Akihiko as the rest. And if marrying the Moon Prince raised his own station in life, well, that wouldn't be so bad, now would it?

Akihiko appreciated the man's humility, and his talent with the flute. And gave him a task as he did the rest. "Bring me an ever-burning rock from Hybernia, the land in the north."

Few had traveled as far as Hybernia. The land was said to be in eternal winter. At the heart of this land is a cauldron of fire, with rocks that give off constant heat, lending the surrounding plateau inhabitable. Endo thought Akihiko was crazy for suggesting he travel to the most northern point of the globe. But no one else had outwardly complained, so he steeled himself for the task.

To cross that far over the oceans required a special passage. Ships required offerings to Kala to ensure a safe journey. It took all of Endo's savings to purchase a ship willing to travel to Hybernia. He gave up his bamboo flute to the ship's altar to Kala.

It took months to sail through the sea and storm to the northernmost continent. The captain and crew promised to wait for him on its cold rocky shores but would not join him on his expedition.

Endo had not planned what to do once he arrived. He had prepared a coat and some rations, and a simple tent, but it was far colder than he expected, and the light was dim, the sun not rising above the horizon. He saw not a single soul as he pushed north, into the wind and the snow. There was no wood for a fire, merely endless rolling hills of snow. He shivered himself to sleep each night, listening to the howling of the wind. The loneliness, cold, and fatigue proved too much. After three days of misery, he turned around and plodded back to the ship.

His fingers and toes were blue and never fully regained their feeling. He spent most of the voyage home burrowed in layers of blankets, drinking hot broth, mumbling to himself.

Akihiko's fourth suitor was Kami, a soldier for the empress. The empress had sent her to evaluate this mysterious Moon Prince's threat level. Kami saw no threat, but did see the potential for power.

Kami bowed to Akihiko, her topknot securely in place. For this meeting, she had changed out of her soldier leathers and wore a soft robe, which she immediately regretted, having nowhere to buckle her knives.

Akihiko's task for her was right down to her expertise. "Bring me a unicorn horn."

Kami's eyes lit up with eagerness. She had never known someone to hunt a unicorn. What a boast that would be. The empress was even willing to fund the research and expedition.

Kami researched in the empress's library, looking through bestiaries. No unicorns lived in Moshotan. The other half of Kenaleko was home to demons and dark spirits, not the pure creatures of light. She would have to travel far to the east, to Kisul, the mythical paradise. The continent was closer by bird flight to the west, but the Razorback Peaks split the earth in two, rising out of the sea in a fearsome, impassable wall, from the southernmost point all the way to Hybernia.

Kami despaired at the expedition it would take to travel through the seas, past Tessagonia, and all the way to Kisul. And then to travel that unmapped land, hunting for a creature of myth, where other unknown creatures dwell, some of which would be a threat to any explorer.

Part of her yearned to take on the task, to claim that glory. But she had a mere seven months to acquire and bring back the unicorn horn. She continued to study the bestiaries further, and found a much more promising solution, another creature with a similar horn. Akihiko surely wouldn't know the difference.

Kami commandeered a whaling vessel with a crew that had experience hunting the narwhals that lived in the colder waters near Hybernia. Kami thrived out at sea, and even learned from the crew when she could. Once they found a pod of the narwhals, she assisted in the effort to capture and kill three of them. They were happy to sell Kami one horn, paid for with the empress's funds, while they kept the meat and blubber.

The last of the suitors was Ayumi. Ayumi's hair was not the traditional black, it was a reddish brown with a light wave. Her family was well enough off that she was allowed time in her youth to daydream in the fields, and her round face had a light dusting of freckles. Her father collected books, so she was also more well-read than most. She had seven siblings, and would escape outdoors or into books to find some peace and quiet. It was her curiosity which brought her to the bamboo cutter's home. So many had flocked by her family estate to see this Moon Prince, like a pilgrimage. She had to see for herself.

While the other suitors sought Akihiko's attention with their musical instruments, or with expensive gifts, Ayumi wrote poetry. She would climb up the bamboo cutter's wall to watch for Akihiko in his garden and compose the verses she would say to him. But she was too shy to send them.

When Akihiko finally welcomed her into his garden, Ayumi blushed fiercely and kept her head down. She felt so plain beside his composed beauty. His pale skin was unmarked by the sun, his hair as black as night, and falling as smooth as silk. New poetry verses filled her mind, as inspired as she was by his beauty. Yet still she could not speak the words, fearing they would fall flat.

Akihiko presented her with a task as he did the others. To bring him a golden phoenix egg from the top of the Razorback Peaks.

Ayumi nodded her consent, still unable to speak.

It was easier to find a ship to sail to the Razorback Peaks than to the other continents. Ayumi took a loan from her father to book passage. For the gift to Kala, she offered a jade tiger figurine that had been a gift from her mother. It took only a week to sail to the Razorback Peaks, the mountain range that divided the world. The jagged spears of rock loomed over the horizon for days. The ship stopped in their shadow, but did not approach the foot.

Ayumi confronted the captain. "I need to climb the mountains. Can't you get any closer?"

"Too dangerous. There are rocks hidden beneath the sea, ready to tear the ships apart." He pointed to wreckage closer to the peaks. As Ayumi looked further, she could see multiple ships torn up on the rocks, from those looking for a passage through to the other side.

Ayumi sighed. "Then lower the rowboat. I'll go further on my own."

"We'll await your return. I'll set a cabin boy with a look-ing-scope to watch for you."

Rowing a boat proved harder than expected, but Ayumi eventu-ally got the hang of it. Her arms tired quickly, but she reached the foot of the peaks before noonday. The mountains were all rock. No soil, no beach to bring her boat aground. She managed to tie her boat off to a pointy rock near a flatter ledge that she hoped to climb onto.

The boat rocked with the waves, and she could not simply step onto the rock as she had hoped. Instead, she leaped, limbs flailing as the boat pushed out under her feet. The ledge was higher than it looked, but she landed with her upper body atop it, knocking the air from her lungs. Her hands scrambled for purchase as she pulled herself onto the ledge. She stood up, wiped her hands on her now torn pantaloons, and studied the mountain in front of her. There were a few likely handholds in reach, but she was no experienced climber.

"This is just like climbing the bamboo cutter's wall. That's all. Just one hand at a time." She steeled herself and reached for the first handhold, then the next. She dug the toe of a boot into a crevice, and again. This wasn't so bad. She could do this. Refusing to look down, she focused on just her hand and foot placement. Her hands were scratched, her knees bruised, but she made it to the next ledge. Only a thousand or so more feet to go. The ledge was barely wide enough to sit on. She braced her back against the cliff wall and looked out. Other than the ship she had come on, the view was entirely ocean. No land in sight. The sun glinted off the waters, blinding her. How was it noon already? She dug in her small pack for a piece of jerky.

A shadow swooped overhead, and she nearly dropped her snack. A large bird, about the size of an eagle, perched on an outcropping of rock a few arm lengths from her. The sunlight glinted on its red and orange feathers, making it seem on fire. A phoenix. The fire bird was real. Legends said the bird dies in fire and is reborn from the ashes.

And this legendary bird was eying her jerky. How could she refuse? Ayumi tossed the meat toward the phoenix, and it caught it in its beak. It cocked its head to the side, then spread its glorious wings and flew off, back to the higher peaks.

What a gift the sight was. Though now she had nothing to eat. And still thousands of feet to climb. The bird may be able to resurrect, but if she fell to the rocky waters below, there would be no coming back. This task was ridiculous and clearly out of her skill level. Akihiko's crazy request was not worth her life.

Ayumi reversed her route and carefully climbed back down the cliff to the safety of the rowboat below. She returned to the ship, and then home.

As it had been less than a month since her last visit, there was still half a year until Akihiko's birthday. Ayumi asked to see him, to tell her tale, but he refused any visitors until the specified date. Without the crowds and suitors crowding the gates, the servants and family were more freely coming and going. As one servant left for the market, Ayumi followed her and struck up a conversation.

The servant was a middle-aged woman, her dark hair streaked with white. She carried a covered basket. The woman glanced over at Ayumi as she approached.

"So sorry to disturb you. You are one of Akihiko's servants, are you not? Perhaps you would be willing to help me."

"You. You are one of those suitors, always hovering outside our gates. You are the reason I have not been out to visit my children. Shouldn't you be out fetching a present for him?"

Ayumi lowered her head in shame. "I already failed my task. I hoped to tell him about my efforts, but they won't let me in before his birthday. I am Ayumi. What is your name?"

The woman sighed and continued walking. "If you wish to speak, then walk with me. I do not wish to be late. I am Yira."

The village bustled as people returned home after a day's work. Ayumi quickened her pace to keep up as they wove through the packed dirt streets. "You mentioned children. Are you visiting them now? How old are they?" She wasn't sure she wanted children of her own. She had a sufficient amount of siblings and a multitude of nieces and nephews. Children wouldn't give her the peace and quiet she craved.

"My three children are all grown. The youngest is about Aki's age and is engaged himself. I'm joining them for dinner to meet his bride-to-be. Aki even sent them a gift, some fine blue silk for their wedding gowns."

"Oh, how lovely." Ayumi remembered that silk; it was one of Seru's gifts for Akihiko. "He knows your children, then?"

"Oh yes. They grew up together. I was Aki's nursemaid. By the time he was weaned, Keizo and Rika kept me on to head the staff of their new household."

"Could you tell me more of Akihiko?"

Yira gave a wistful smile. "It is sad that you are the first of the suitors to ask. Most just want to look, they don't truly want to know him. He's just a prize to be won." She shifted the basket to her other hip and looked thoughtful. "Aki treated my children as equals. He was a quiet child. He gave off a calm aura. Whenever my children cried or quarreled, I would take them for a visit and soon everything would be peaceful again. That alone would have been payment enough to stay on with the household. He rarely asks the servants to do things for him, preferring to work with his own hands, clean his own room. When Aki isn't in his meditation garden, he is likely playing the harp or reading."

It sounded like Akihiko was as beautiful on the inside as he was on the outside. Ayumi's mind wandered, picturing the two of them reading together in his meditation garden.

Yira bumped Ayumi with her basket, interrupting the pleasant daydream. They had stopped in front of a lovely two-story house of the precious, red-streaked tiger wood. "This is where I leave you. Thank you for the conversation. It made the walk feel easier. Good luck with your courtship, Ayumi."

3

On the day of Akihiko's twenty-first birthday, the five suitors were brought inside the bamboo cutter's home to wait together in an antechamber. The spacious room had plenty of plush seating, but the suitors all huddled in the middle in anticipation. Endo, Shotaro, Kami, and Seru each showed off their wondrous gifts, bragging of their trials, and each claiming they worked harder and had the best gift. Seeing all the wondrous items, Ayumi separated herself from the group, knowing she had failed Akihiko and had no object of his desire. All she had brought was a single piece of paper. She found herself clenching it in her fist and smoothed it back out.

Each suitor was brought before Akihiko one at a time. None got to see his reaction to the others, and they did not return to the same room after.

Seru presented her gift, the jeweled branch. "As you asked, a branch from the Gloaming Realm. I traveled deep in their realm, past underwater lakes, avoiding fae and creatures in the shadows with glowing red eyes. As you said, there was a tree of silver, gold, and diamond."

Akihiko took the branch. "It is a lovely and delicate thing." He broke the fruit off its stem with an audible snap. "This must be the fabled ambrosia fruit, then." Seru cringed as Akihiko attempted to bite into the fruit. The gold was soft enough that his teeth left a dent, but it was evident that it was pure golden metal, and not simply golden colored fruit. He tossed the false branch and fruit to the ground. A deceiver, Seru was banished from the bamboo cutter's land. Most of her own wealth was lost to pay her debtors, those artisans that had spent so many months making her false gift.

Shotaro proudly presented Akihiko with the dragon pearl, a shimmering orb the size of his own head. He spun a tale about a long voyage at sea, and a desperate hunt for the sea dragon. He worked in all the details about ships and whale hunting that he had to listen to.

Akihiko gently took the orb. "This is large, for a heart. Must have been quite the dragon."

"Oh, it was indeed! Took out three of our crew before we could subdue it and cut out its heart."

The Moon Prince turned and stepped into the deeper shadows of the bamboo grove and sighed. "There is just one problem. A real dragon pearl would glow in the dark." He threw the orb to the flagstone path and it shattered into the clay pieces it was.

In shame, Shotaro retreated home, but news of his deceit and cowardice had already reached his family, and they did not welcome him back. He lived the rest of his life alone in a small hut deep in the woods.

Not to be shown up, Endo also turned up to Akihiko's birthday with a gift. In an iron pot, he presented a burning stone. He shared his tale of sea travel, and the cold, bitter north. Leaving out the part of his premature departure, he claimed he traveled to the cauldron of fire, where plants grew, and people lived, and how they were gracious to award him with a single burning stone to warm his return journey.

Akihiko warmed his hands over the burning rock. "What a wonderful gift that would be. However..." He dumped the rock into the pond, where it quickly went out, as the lump of coal it clearly was. "A true ever-burning stone would not be put out by mere pond water. You have failed and lied as the others. Go."

Endo was free to return to his farm, but the lack of feeling in his digits made work hard, and he could no longer play music. He retired to the warmest part of the island, but forever felt a chill in his bones.

When Kami presented Akihiko with the spiraling horn, she spun tales of traveling to Kisul and hunting the jungles, avoiding predators, and finding a unicorn in a magical glade.

Akihiko sent a servant to bring a specially prepared tea and two cups. Another servant brought out a small tea table and two stools. Akihiko thanked the servants and gestured for Kami to sit across from him. He took the horn and dipped it into the tea, stirred it for a moment, then set the horn on the table. He poured out the tea into the two cups. "This is nightshade tea. Very poisonous. However, a unicorn horn will purify anything it touches. So, drink up."

Kami had lifted her cup but paled at the words. She threw the full cup to the ground. "Don't drink that. It's a narwhal horn. No true magic."

Akihiko sighed and set his own cup back on the table. "As I suspected. Your hubris could have killed us both."

The empress, having learned where her funding went, banished Kami from her service.

Kami realized that she wanted adventure more than marriage, and her empress's favor was more important to her than Akihiko's. She began preparations for a true trip to Kisul, to impress the empress with the fame of being the first to kill a unicorn.

As Ayumi had been last to receive her task, she was last to be summoned before Akihiko. Alone in the room, she sat on a bench in the corner, willing herself to keep breathing. She dreaded Akihiko's reaction to her failure.

A servant came in and stopped at the site of the waiting Ayumi. "Is this courtship business still not done?"

Ayumi looked up at Yira, the servant she had spoken to before. Yira scanned her face, then came to sit beside her, reaching up to wipe away tears Ayumi hadn't noticed falling. "Oh, I know you! What troubles you, girl?"

"What if Akihiko doesn't want to see me? I'm just going to disappoint him. I should leave before he calls me."

Yira leaned close and whispered, "Let me tell you a secret. I saw some of the other suitors on their way out. None of them looked happy."

"How does that help me?"

"That means you still have a chance. So go in there and let Akihiko see you. Not just this," she gestured up and down to Ayumi's form, "but this," she said, placing her hand over Ayumi's heart.

After Yira left, Ayumi rehearsed what she would say to Akihiko. It seemed an eternity before the servant returned to escort her to the meditation garden. He sat on his smooth rock. It seemed the previous gifts had all been cleared out and stored in another room. Ayumi's hands shook as she stood before the Moon Prince.

She waited, but he said nothing, simply nodded up at her. Ayumi took a deep breath. "You tasked me with bringing you a phoenix egg. I traveled to the Razorback Peaks, where they nest. But the rocks were too sharp and steep. I was unable to climb the mountain. I saw a phoenix, but no nest. I have failed you." Her voice wavered. "I did not want to return without a gift. As such, I have written a poem. If you will hear it."

Akihiko's face was still and unreadable. After a moment, he nodded again, gesturing for her to continue.

Ayumi closed her eyes for a moment and breathed deep, feeling the air fill her. In the stillness, she could feel the calmness that Yira had mentioned. Ayumi relaxed into the peace that Akihiko radiated. Hands steadier, and stomach settled, she opened her eyes and recited the poem by memory.

> "Earth burning, ashes
> fill the sky until it rains-
> ready for rebirth.

> Lone egg bursts open;
> red wings flutter in new air.
> Phoenix is reborn."

She allowed herself to look into Akihiko's eyes. They were a steady blue pool, filling with tears.

He stood and wiped his eyes. "Thank you, Ayumi. I saw the phoenix clearly with your words. And do not think you have failed me. I gave each of you an impossible task, expecting you to fail. The others brought false artifacts. You brought me the greatest gift, that of truth. I honor that much more than a phoenix egg. I accept your offer of courtship."

One year later, Akihiko announced his engagement to Ayumi. By this point, the entire household had grown fond of the quiet, studious woman. The couple was oft comfortable sharing silence, whereas most would feel a need to fill it.

They planned a simple wedding in the bamboo grove, near to where Keizo had found a babe in a bamboo shoot. Surrounding them were Ayumi's large family, Akihiko's parents, and the household staff that had been as family to Akihiko.

As Akihiko took Ayumi's hands in his, preparing to exchange vows, a light came down from the heavens, overshadowing even Akihiko's glow. Everyone shielded their eyes. When the light dimmed to a manageable level, two people stood at the head of the clearing beside the engaged couple. A man with a mane of bright red hair, and a woman with long black hair and features much like Akihiko. The woman's eyes filled with tears and she reached out both hands to embrace the couple's hands in hers.

"My son. I am Delwyn, Moon Goddess, and this is your father Bentos, Sun God." Keizo and the other guests fell to their knees in awe. Ayumi paled, but Delwyn's grip on her hands kept her aloft.

Delwyn lifted one hand to place it on Akihiko's cheek. "We left you here to protect you, safe from those who would try to steal your power while you were young and vulnerable. We could not raise you in our home in the sky, as you would not age in our realm.

"I was pleased to see you fall in love. I come with both an invitation and a warning. We would like you to return home with us. But the Sky Realm is no place for a mortal. If you choose to bring Ayumi with you, she will not become sick or grow cold or hunger. She will not visibly age, but she will die; not soon, you would still have decades together. But over time, the Sky Realm weakens the mortal heart. And there would be no children. A deity and a mortal cannot bear offspring."

Akihiko gazed into his beloved's eyes. "You have not spoken of wanting children... The choice is yours. Would you give that chance up to join me, spend the rest of your life with me?"

Ayumi nodded. "I have never seen myself as a mother. I would be happy spending the rest of my life with you wherever you choose to dwell."

Akihiko looked back to his father, not this god who had made him, but the man who had raised him. "What of my parents, Keizo and Rika? Could they live with us?"

"We are eternally grateful to them for raising you. However, they would not be able to come with you. They are too old; their hearts are not strong enough. But you could watch over them."

"They do not have many years left. I would rather stay near them."

Bentos proposed a compromise. "You are not human and will never truly be a part of their world." He gestured to the mountain that had watched over Akihiko all his life. "The mountain here rises high enough to touch our realm. You could live there and bridge both realms."

Thus Akihiko, a true Moon Prince, not just in name, married Ayumi, and moved atop Mount Ojai. Delwyn offered to build them a palace, but they opted for a humbler home, surrounded by lush gardens and bamboo groves. Once a year, they came down to visit Keizo and Rika, until the elderly couple passed peacefully together in their sleep, having lived well-fulfilled and happy lives. Akihiko bestowed the estate to Ayumi's family. With his parents gone, Akihiko freely travelled to the Sky Realm to spend time with his parents and his muse sisters, but the land of Kenaleko still had his heart, and he kept his quiet home atop Mount Ojai.

The Moon Prince continues to watch over his people. Shrines were built to honor him, and one can visit when in need of calm and peace.

Author's Note

The Moon Prince is based on a Japanese folktale, The Bamboo
Cutter. It is also known as The Tale of Princess Kaguya (highly
recommend the Studio Ghibli film). I gender swapped the main
character, and added some bisexual representation bringing suitors of both genders. As in the original tale, a bamboo cutter finds
a baby in the grove (I made mine a large bamboo shoot rather
than a tiny baby in a stalk. That part is weird to me.). Many
of the base elements are the same – childless couple, gifts in the
bamboo stalks, baby grows to great beauty, hiding from suitors,
five persistent suitors, and five impossible tasks. In the original,
Kaguya doesn't want to get married at all, and wants her suitors
to fail. I chose to go a different route. Akihiko still expects failure,
but he wants to see who can be honest about it. Many of the tasks
mirror the original in some way as well.

This story really made me sit down and figure out Love with
a Deity. Did I want little demigods running about? Did I want to
make love interests immortal? But then why are the muses still
single? What is it like for a mortal to live in the Sky Realm? I
ended up going with the harder option for the mortal: no children,
shorter lifespan. Have to really choose the life.

This is our first time going beyond the seas, with a glimpse
at other continents beyond Tessagonia. We have Kenaleko to the

west (inspired by East Asia). Hybernia to the north, a land of ever winter. Kisul to the East, a paradise land of mythical creatures. And a world split by a great mountain range.[1] I got to draw a (very crude) map. Someday I will hire out a professional for a nicer version to share.

Timeline wise, this is a direct follow up to *The Gloaming Realm*, following the thread of the brother taken to be raised beyond the seas.

---

1. Look up images for the Dolomites for some of my inspiration.

Thanks for reading

If you have a moment, please review *Tales of Tessagonia: Books 1-6* on your preferred platform.

Want more? My monthly newsletter will bring you updates on my current projects and alert you to new releases. Fantasy, fairytales, poetry, and enchantment.

Join my mailing list now for a free short story:

https://www.briarbooklane.com/mary-w-jensen-newsletter

Acknowledgements

Writing is often a solitary job, but getting it ready for the world is not.

Thank you to my husband, Jeff, for supporting me in this writing and business venture.

Thank you to my wonderful beta readers, Elizabeth and Anika. I appreciate all your insightful feedback and your enthusiasm. My writing is better for it.

Thank you to my coworkers at the library for listening to my writing updates and following my journey.

And thank you to my readers. I hope you have enjoyed this book, and continue to escape into the world of Tessagonia as I have more tales to tell.

About the author

Mary W. Jensen lives in Utah with her husband and son. Mary is the middle of nine children, and escaped the loudness of reality by immersing herself in books and poetry. From chaos comes creation. She is the author of the Tales of Tessagonia series, fairytale novellas set in a shared world, and the poetry book *Chiaroscuro*. Her poetry has been published in the webzines *Moon Drenched Fables*, *Abyss & Apex*, and *Snapdragon Journal*. She is also co-author of the poetry book *Lifelines* by The Poetic Muselings.

You can find Mary online at BriarbookLane.com.

Also by Mary W. Jensen

Tales of Tessagonia Series

The Blazing Princess
Mirror
The Princess Test
Venom and Shadow
The Gloaming Realm
The Moon Prince

Poetry

Chiaroscuro